SLAVE GIRLS
OF ROME

SLAVE GIRLS OF ROME

DON WINSLOW

THIS REVISED AND EXPANDED EDITION WAS WRITTEN EXCLUSIVELY FOR

BLUE MOON BOOKS
AN IMPRINT OF RUNNING PRESS

Contents

"'No woman,' it is said, 'knows truly what she is until she has worn the collar.' Some free women apparently fear sex because they feel it lowers the woman. This is quite correct. In few, if any, human relationships is there perfect equality. The subtle tensions of dominance and submission, universal in the animal world, remain ineradicably, in our blood; they may be thwarted and frustrated but, thwarted and frustrated, they will remain. It is the nature of the male, among mammals, to dominate, that of the female to submit."

—John Norman, *Marauders of Gor*

SLAVE GIRLS OF ROME

Chapter One

A MODEST ORGY

"Rome has become nothing but a rich man's whore," Lucius' drunken mutterings rang in my ears, as I trudged through the streets of the sodden Army camp on that fateful morning. It had rained the day before. Then it got cold. And now the mud was hard, semi-frozen in the cold morning air of autumn. The morning mist that still clung to the hills had not yet been driven away by the sun's early light. There was a definite chill in the heavy air, but I breathed it in deeply, gulping it down, letting my lungs get their fill. The new day did much to clear my head. In spite of the wine, I hadn't slept well last night, but now I felt much better, my spirits improved for the first time in months. I pulled my cloak together, and with renewed determination, turned towards the garrison's headquarters.

We had spent the night carousing at the house of Quintus Licus, a fabulously wealthy merchant who occasionally invited a few of us "Defenders of the Empire" to his pala-tial estate for one of his endless stream of "celebrations." I should add that this was not one of his legendary orgies that you may have heard about. Those went on for days and were justifiably renown throughout the seven hills. Junior officers were never invited to those events, although occasionally our general might find himself among that privileged elite. No, it was to the more modest affairs that we were invited, along with the lesser lights of Roman society —functionaries and various officials who might someday be of use in one of Licus' many schemes.

It was perhaps a measure of our lowly status that our host didn't even bother to grace this august gathering with his presence, but left his social obligations to his wife. The Lady would be our hostess—seeing that the guests were greeted, and their needs met, *all* their needs. And if those guests included a few handsome young officers from the garrison, then his wife, Lydia, a brash, bawdy woman with big floppy tits and a loud braying voice, would be only too happy to see to her obligations. The Lady's appetite was insatiable; her propensity for enjoying the weapons of hardy soldiers was legendary. The nickname she has earned in the officer's mess, "Labia," seemed apt. Even now she watched us with half-lidded eyes from her vantage point on the low couch at the far end of the room; easing back the slippery gown of the finest green silk, cut fashionably low in front so that her tits threatened to spill out at the slightest movement. The gown's hem was casually exposing the entire lengths of her legs, and she left it where it lay, shamelessly crossing the very top of her robust thighs. From time to time the lady would smilingly nod her approval of the merry crowd, waving a ring-bejeweled hand; her heavily painted lips would crease into a lewd, come-hither grin whenever a young officer happened to glance her way.

She licked her lips, half rising from the couch, the gleam of lust flaring in her dark eyes, when Gaius, deciding to get more comfortable, unbuckled his belt and slipped off his tunic, to recline once again, bare-chested now and clad in nothing but his linen loincloth. I nudged Lucius who took one look at the leering lady and whispered with an ominous groan that now no one would be safe! And I am certain that the matron's attentions would have been lavished upon us, had not she, just at that moment, been diverted by her attending slave. This pretty tousle-haired lad had been kneeling on the floor beside her couch, and was engaged in licking and kissing his mistress' shapely legs, making his way assiduously from her bare feet along their smooth lengths. And just at the moment when she sat up on one elbow, the pleasuring tongue slithered inside her upper thighs, to find a place where it caused the lady to gasp, and then collapse back in weak disarray onto the satiny cushions. Her thick lashes fluttered and her kohl-lidded eyes slid closed, her gleaming lips curling in a smile of dreamy ecstasy, as the purposeful head continued its journey between her legs, disappearing under the loose folds of that slippery gown. Her hands came down to find and guide that tousled head burrowing forward in dutiful exploration. The Mistress of the House of Licus would be kept busy for some time.

And so we safely turned our attention way from our preoccupied hostess, and prepared to lounge about on the thick silken pillows, giving ourselves up to the tender ministrations of our absent host's charming slave girls, nubile young serving wenches, who pranced half-naked, wearing nothing but the briefest of skirts low on their hips as they scurried about to serve their master's guests.

Lucius was quite taken with a long-haired girl who moved about us with her flagon of wine; a nicely-curved

lass with flaring hips and proud jaunty tits. When he beckoned to her, she hastened across the room, naked titties
bouncing in the most delightful way. And when she bent
over to fill his cup, those full breasts hung down heavily,
moving in a seductive sway before his wondering eyes — the
girl, perhaps inadvertently, moving forward to offer him
those succulent fruits, a tempting handful of which no man
could possibly refuse. Lucius reached up to help himself,
loosely capturing a dangling tit, balancing it for a moment
on his curved palm and studying it. Then taking the wide
fleshy tip between his fingers, he began idly toying with the
conveniently-placed nipple, whilst expounding on his views
to us. He kept the poor girl like that, half bent over. And as
he played with the plaything of the rich man, his voice
became a bit sad, wistful perhaps at the injustice of it all. We
were but soldiers of Rome and though he might borrow such
pleasures, they could never be his to have and own: the rich
opulence of his surroundings, the hoard of beautiful slave
girls owned by such a crass, money-grubbing trader.

Not that Lucius was poor, far from it, for he came from
one of Rome's most prominent families and, like most of my
brother officers, he was provided with a generous allowance
which far overshadowed his meager army pay, even if his
family's wealth was not on the massive scale of our host's
legendary millions. Alas, I was even less fortunate than
Lucius. The son of an honest but poor farmer, I joined the
Legions at sixteen, and had learned early on to take my pleasure wherever I could find it. Two days after payday, I would
inevitably find myself reduced to the whores who were kept
at the barracks for the use of the troops. Thus, I too leapt at
this invitation, only too ready to take advantage of Licus'
"generosity," and ease back on the chair, opening my knees

to invite, the comely lass who knelt at my chair to have her way with my staunchly erect manhood.

By now, my companions were well occupied. Lucius was avidly exploring the writhing young body of the long-haired slave girl, while Gaius was dallying with an olive-skinned girl with plump tits and dusky nipples whom he held perched on his lap. Looking down on the young girl on her knees before me, I let my eyes appreciate the willowy lines of her lean body, those slender shoulders, with small pancake tits that seemed to be emerging from that maidenly, flat chest. The slave girl's fresh, expectant face was surrounded by a mane of thick auburn hair, tawny tresses that hung loosely down to halo her delicate shoulders.

I saw the question in her eyes as she edged forward, and nodded my permission for her to begin; immediately the vixen's smile widened. Eagerly, she reached for me, brushing back my loincloth, which by this time was all I wore, freeing my stiffened penis to spring up hopefully before her big brown eyes. A shiver of delight raced through my tense body as the girl's small fingers traced my naked manhood, closed on my upright prick.

I watched through half-lidded eyes, as she shifted back to sit on folded legs all the while holding my taut sex so lightly in those cool soft hands. With a sure delicate touch, the talented girl teased up and down my shaft, tracing my fierce erection with the pads of her fingertips. I clenched my teeth against the maddening rise of pleasure. Her adept fingers curved around the shaft and used those talons to lightly scratch along the smooth hardened length. I heard myself groan at the fluttering teasing of those delightfully cool fingers when they slipped up between my legs to softly cradle my the hairy sack of my balls. The slave girl's supple fingers cupped my scrotum; and gave a little squeeze to my masculine equipment before she began gently rolling my testicles in the palm of her hand. I sighed with contentment and let my eyes close, giving myself up to the heavenly touch.

With one hand still cupping my balls, she now brought the other into play, wrapping nimble fingers around the turgid shaft, squeezing lightly, tightening her little fist till she held me in an iron grip and she had me groaning and twisting in her hands. I managed to open my eyes enough to look down on the top of her head and watch her as she leaned forward, bringing her pursed lips closer so that I thrilled at the feel of her hot breath sweeping over the throbbing prick that hovered just before her face. Slowly, she extended her flickering tongue until the very tip touched the sensitive underside just below the crown of my upright prick. I clenched my fists and whimpered like a little boy, craning back at the piercing thrill generated by the feel of that wet, tantalizing tongue as it lightly fluttered along the underside of my straining manhood.

Switching tactics, this talented slave flattened her tongue and licked with broad wet strokes, lapping up the length, swirling around the ridge of the crown then slithering down to the base. And there she would lightly nibble at the root of the shaft, soaking my pubic hair. Her velvety tongue slid wetly, lavishly, all over my scrotum, till her small head was burrowing between my legs, her probing tongue searching for my perineum and once there she crouched down and stretched up awkwardly to bury her face between my thighs, electrifying me with jolting thrills as she pressed nose and lips and chin into my crotch.

I couldn't stand much more of this exquisite pleasure; my hands reached out to grab and extract the girl's burrowing head. When she came up for air, she went immediately back to the shaft, lightly holding it in both hands licking greedily, lapping generously all along its length till my upstanding cock was glistening with the sheen of her saliva.

Curving my hands to lightly cradle her head, I ran my fingers through the thick head of hair, luxuriating in the silky tresses. Tightening my grip, I held her head rigidly still while I rubbed my super-ready cock all over her pretty face. Then I let her eager lips nibble on me, guiding her up and down my straining manhood, letting her lick her way almost to the top, but keeping her from reaching the sensitive underside just below the crown.

I heard my own whimpers coming as from a distance as delicious waves of pure pleasure welled up in me, drowning out all else, as the slave girl continued her obsequious devotion, methodically covering every inch, working me over with avid lips and agile tongue, until she had me squirming helplessly, uncontrollably, driven to distraction by the exquisite feel of that unrelenting tongue action. The feel of that lavish tongue sliding wetly up and down my shaft was so exquisite I couldn't help moaning, tossing my head back and lifting my loins towards her till I was arching my back as though offering her even more, wanting her to take my lust-swollen sex even more deeply into her hot little mouth. I arched my back, my eyes fluttered closed; a groan escaped my tightly-pressed lips as I surrendered to the delicious waves of pleasure this sensual young woman was generating in my groin.

Then the tickling play of that lively tongue stopped, and when I looked down at her through half-lidded eyes, it was to see her reach out to grab me, and tilt the rigid shaft towards her as she bent down to slowly take my cock in her receptive mouth. Inch by inch, that marvelous girl took me in, sliding the taut ring of her lips down the swollen shaft, ducking her head to so eagerly go down on me. Looking down on her through narrowed eyes I watched the top of her small head as it bobbed up and down in smooth easy rhythm.

With surprising skill my darling little felliatrix was sucking me off, her cheeks hollowing out, as she vacuumed me with ruthless determination. I groaned, clamping my hands on her thin naked shoulders and held on, tightening my grip, clenching my teeth as the most excruciating waves of pleasure rocketed through me. Then the clever slave girl added a new thrill. She never stopped her energetic sucking, but now she began to bring her tongue up, swirling it around in an upward spiral each time she came up. The novel sensation instantly drove me to new heights of pleasure, it was a pleasure that was almost painful, unbearable, straining my endurance to its absolute limits as I held on, arching my rigid hips high into the air, clinging, with gritted teeth, to the last shreds of control.

But the powerful upsurge in my loins became irresistible under the sheer intensity of the repeated thrills, thrills that escalated wildly, till they sent me careening towards the supreme moment of climax. I could hold out no longer. My last conscious act was to push the eager girl back, extracting my throbbing penis, and aiming it right at her flushed, excited face. At that exact moment I exploded in a tremendous climax sending a powerful surge of sperm erupting from the pulsating shaft to splatter that pretty face. Then I was coming with furious urgency, spurting thick wads of semen that jetted out to decorate another man's slave girl, painting her neat features with ropy strands of thick creamy sperm in furious pulsations that seemed to go on and on and on.

Chapter Two

THE CALL OF THE NORTH

Even before Lucius had given words to my feelings, I had learned that for a poor but ambitious junior officer, the legion's permanent barracks, situated as they were just outside of Rome, could not be considered the most hospitable of postings. And if that officer gambled a bit too much, and was heavily in debt, his plight was even worse. I was restless, increasingly desperate, hating my poverty, and thoroughly bored with the dull routine of camp life in the peacetime Army. It was a few days earlier when I had been ruminating about my fate that I happened upon a slave caravan. Such long lines of fresh captives were quite common in Rome in those days. Day or night, one could find them bound for the slave markets, wending their ways through the streets of that decadent city, a city insatiable for ever more human flesh.

Now I watched as two long rows of dusty naked captives, at first, only men, trudged past me. Their eyes downcast, their tread slow and dull. It was easy to see from their long unkempt hair, powerful builds, and scarred, hard-muscled bodies, that these must have been barbarian fighters, once proud warriors whose spirit had been broken by defeat at the hands of Rome's invincible legions. Now, they were being led by the overseers, who found no need to use their whips on their dazed and beaten captives. The shuffling men moved their feet mindlessly, hands manacled before them, chained to one another in loose coffles of eight men each.

There were lines of captured women, too. And although these were fewer, I studied them with much greater interest. Many were stocky, heavily built barbarian women, clearly destined to end up as field slaves, or at best, house slaves, although occasionally one found the kind of well-made body that might elevate its fortunate owner to work in the bedchamber or in one of the city's pleasure houses. The long lines of would-be slaves were broken by the occasional slaver's wagon, the kind with the large wheels and wide flatbeds that held standing captives in tall barred cages. The wagons were reserved for captured nobles or for those women who were fated to become specially trained sex slaves, since it was felt unwise to wear out the more valuable merchandise by the rigors of a long exhausting march to Rome.

I watched the sorry parade without much interest as it made its way slowly by, when a creaking wagon came into view, and with it, a particularly rare prize. The jogging cage held a breath-taking statuesque blond girl. She must be a captive from the Northern peoples, I realized, a rare Teuton to be sure, as I recognized the striking Nordic features that Gaius had once described to me in such loving detail. This Germanic beauty was impressively tall, regal in bearing; her sculpted features so elegantly made that I could only stare in awe. Most of those favored captives who found themselves so displayed in the tall wooden cages would shrink back to huddle in a far corner averting their eyes, or they might squat down studying the planks on the floor with head held low in the utter shame of defeat. But this woman did no such thing!

This regal beauty stood naked, yet in bold defiance, her cold blue eyes squarely meeting those of her Roman enemies, her strong legs set in a widened stance to compensate for the swaying roll of the wagon. Her hands clasped the bars at either side of her pale face, and as she stood regarding the rabble, there was nothing but icy contempt for those who would seek to subdue her. I had to have her!

Enthralled, I studied that magnificent, naked body, the lean hard muscles tapering in long feminine contours, the breasts, firm, high set, hard, and fiercely proud with prominent pink nipples that seemed to jut straight out in open defiance. My eyes fell to the silvery fleece of her brazen womanhood, a triangle of soft wispy curlings that thickened at the apex into a blond tuft only half hiding the pouting cuntlips. Her fuzzy pubic hair was paler than the hair on her head; the latter was long and thick, and gave a hint of former glories. Now, it was matted and unkempt so it gave her the frazzled look of a wild woman. I wondered if her new owner would have sense enough to allow the girl to keep that long mane of pure blond gold, or would he insist she be shorn, reduced to the sort of blond stubble that many citizens thought quite fashionable for their slaves these days.

As the last of the train passed by, I found myself following the parade to the slave market, eager to see if this

Nordic goddess would be placed on the block today. Such a splendid Teutonic specimen would certainly fetch a healthy price from any of a dozen of the best known procurers, but it was more likely that some wealthy patron would pay dearly to add this exquisite beauty to his private collection. Of course, there was no way I could even dream of buying such a woman myself, having but two coins in my purse at the time. That was out of the question!

Still, I was intrigued, hopelessly taken by her. I wanted in the worst way to see her standing alone on the raised platform: a splendid nude, presented in all her naked glory for public inspection, posed for the edification of the rabble of Rome. Would her regal demeanor falter when this strong proud female stood poised to meet her fate? Would the look of sullen defiance in those remote blue eyes give way to fear when she found herself naked and alone on the raised platform before the lusty, bawdy, raucous crowd that inevitably gathered to rake in the free public spectacles the slave auctions provided?

The destination of this sorry parade was the grounds of largest and best of the pubic auctions run by two brothers named Maximus. By the time I got there a good-sized crowd was already on hand, with more joining every minute. Today's slaves were being lined up, connecting tethers undone so that they might mount the auction block singly, one by one, to be present themselves, to be inspected, and ultimately sold to the highest bidder. The slaves' manacles were removed, and before they ascended the raised platform, a high leather collar was fixed around each neck. A thin rawhide strip attached to the collar was used as a lead so that the handler might bring the slave forward to be presented.

By now the captives would be properly cowed so that the heavier whip that was used in the early days of captivity, and retained for the most recalcitrant, could easily be dispensed with for this lot. To keep their charges in line the more skillful handlers need only employ a thin hickory stick.

The pace was smooth and business-like. Each slave was made to mount the steps and there to suffer the indignities of being closely examined by the chief auctioneer, one of the Maximus brothers, who conducted the sort of thorough inspection one would expect to see if he were buying a valuable racing horse. Once he was well satisfied, the auctioneer would set the starting price, and the bidding could begin.

I recognized this particular fellow: a skinny, bald gnome named Glutus, and I watched the obvious pleasure he took in his task, laughing when I saw the leer than came over his lips, as he contemplated the pleasure of having such pretty women about to be placed in his hands. On the lookout for the slightest show of defiance, he stepped forward, eager to make this sorry lot do his bidding, adopting all sorts of poses to show off their best features while he went over the fine merchandise meticulously with his hands, lingering especially with the females, feeling here and there, probing this crevice, or squeezing that jutting curve. The man obviously loved his work!

Bidding that day was hot and heavy, and the line moved quickly. I pushed my way through the crowd, eager to see more as her time drew near, and the big blonde moved to the head of the line to have her manacles removed. She stood with eyes front, ignoring the rough handler who fitted the high leather collar around her neck, then paused to run his callused hand down over her left breast, copping a quick feel, before he busied himself with attaching the rawhide lead. Now the tall stately blonde was led to the wooden steps.

The burly handler held the girl's lead in one hand while in the other he loosely carried a thin pliant rod, no thicker than a man's finger at the blunt end and tapering to a point at the other. He wielded the rod skillfully, careful to use it only on the fleshy hindquarters of the more attractive slaves, so as not to damage that valuable property. He was not a particularly cruel man, but he was an impatient one, and I saw a flick of the wrist and the girl's hips jerked forward as the whippy rod solidly struck her handsome rump, impelling her to step lively in spite of herself. He led the naked young woman up the steps and brought her to the center of the high square platform, and the crowd seemed to quiet down as though sensing something special was about to take place.

"Stand at attention! Hands together, behind your neck! Elbows back . . . head up!" Glutus snapped, stepping up to the tall blonde till he was close to but not touching her, to stand with his eyes just inches from the side of her expressionless face, coolly appraising her beauty, those long clean lines.

At first the blond barbarian didn't move a muscle, but a sharp whack on the bare bottom reminded her of the importance of instant obedience. Her shoulders shot up in abrupt recoil and she turned to look at her handler with a look of utter disdain. But the wicked rod in his hand only rose slightly, and it was enough to cause her to turn back resentfully and to slowly bring up her arms to assume the mandated pose, throwing back her shoulders, proudly thrusting out her firm breasts, locking her eyes on some distant horizon. There was a lively murmur of approval from the crowd.

The lecherous old goat licked his chops as he passed his hands up and down that magnificent body, feeling the captive woman up freely, lavishly savoring feminine curves and contours, caressing the rich handfuls of both breasts, pausing briefly to sample her taut nipples before slipping his hands between her legs to fondle the soft folds of her blond sex. He stepped behind her, ran his hands up and down her sleek haunches, greedily exploring each mound and crevice of that splendid perfectly-still nude. He looked in her eyes, had her open her mouth, pressed back her lips to study her strong clenched teeth.

Then the meticulous auctioneer stepped back, preparing to put the big nude through her paces. He had her widen her stance, and then drop her arms and lean forward with head raised and hands placed just above the knees, so that the rich full breasts swung forward to hang in two succulent tit-bags, while she looked out over her audience. Now, he brought up his pointed stick, and used it to trace a line up the side of her curved body, starting at the nearest sturdy thigh, moving up over the generous cradle of her hip, then onward up her flank, till the traveling point slid around under her bent torso and found a dangling tit. He used the stick to stir the helpless woman's tits, flicking them up so they juddered most delightfully, as a titter of laughter ran through the crowd. He traced a line from under the hanging sacks over a now hard yet pliant nipple, and up the slope outlining the generous curve of ripe feminine pulchritude.

A nod to his assistant had that stocky man step up and grab a fistful of the blond hair at the back of the girl's head, to yank back her neck, forcing his captive to raise her shoulders and deepen the curve in her back. And then, while she was being held like that, she was ordered to bring her hands up to cup her ample breasts, as if offering them to the hungry audience. She obeyed, her eyes daring them to look; the gesture got an immediate roar of lusty approval.

Now her tormentor used the pointy rod to toy with the proffered tits. The devilish instrument pressed in, indenting the soft flesh, testing the resiliency of the breast, the softness of the enticing flesh, the underlying firmness. He spent a long time teasing her nipples, moving from one to the other, scratching lightly at the hardening points, then flicking the little pliant tip that seemed to stand up so hopefully under the mild stimulation till he had the big, pink nipples blossoming. Another roar of approval swept though the restless crowd.

I marveled at the girl's control as she held herself perfectly still while the wicked pointer invited the crowd to appreciate the strength of those long, finely-muscled legs, and those robust thighs. Thoroughly enjoying himself, Glutus was clearly playing to the excited mob. After a few minutes if this, he had her drop her arms to resume the starting position, commanding her to rise up to her full height, and stand once more at attention, hands loosely at her sides, legs rigidly together. Then he had the young woman turn around so that her back was towards the audience and we were greeted by our first view of the long gently sloping back, and the comely form of that shapely rearend. Looking closely one could make out two faint pink welts that crossed the buttocks, traces of the whippy rod that had been so smartly laid across her bottom earlier.

The pointer traced down her back and over the twin swells of that womanly, high-set bottom.

Curtly, she was ordered to bend down once more, assuming the same pose as before, but this time turned with her back to us, so that she was offering up her jutting behind to be admired. Not quite satisfied with the results, the auctioneer forced the girl to bend down even lower, arching her back with hands braced on her thighs, thus boldly trusting back that choice, rounded rump of hers. His next command must have been even more obscene, even more humiliating, for this time the proud barbarian shook her blond mane in mute refusal. Like lightening, the whippy rod shot out to whack her crisply across the tautly-drawn curves of her jutting butt, causing the bending girl to jerk upward, her hands flying back to her tightened cheeks at the viciousness of the stinging lick. It was enough to prompt her to readily obey even the most perverse demands placed upon her, as we saw, as next she responded by squirming her hips and shaking her tail from side to side in a delightfully provocative gesture. Waves of raucous laughter greeted the sight of this proud Teutonic woman wiggling her ass like a Babylonian whore!

To add even further to her humiliation, the poor girl was next made to rotate her behind in a lewdly suggestive manner, eliciting a spate of bawdy offers from the increasingly excited rabble. After a few minutes of this amusing diversion, her tormentor allowed her to straighten up, but it was only so she could be put in an even more humiliating pose. For now he had her turn around once more to face the mob. She stood before them with chin held high; her blond face, expressionless. She stood there: a big blond animal, powerful and deeply sensual, and still able to hold herself coldly remote in spite of the lewd poses she was forced to endure for the pleasure of her masters.

Cautioning her to keep her hands on her hips, and hold herself perfectly erect, he ordered his captive to her knees. The pointed wand was used to nudge her knees apart, giving us an unhindered view of the blond fleece of her vulva. In the most humiliating gesture of sexual sub-servience he had her reach down and pry open the thick lips of her vagina to show her gaping sex to the cheering multitude. The crowd went wild!

After exhibiting herself for what must have seemed like forever to her, the kneeling woman was allowed to rise up and resume the first pose: hands clasped behind her neck. The bidding was about to begin. At last, satisfied that he knew he value of what he had, the wily auctioneer stepped back, mounted his podium and announced the starting price. The sum he mentioned to begin the bidding for this proud beauty, took my breath away, and got an audible gasp of admiration from the gaping crowd. And that was only where the brisk bidding *started!*

After that day I couldn't get the powerful image of that big blonde out of my mind. It stayed with me by day, and it haunted my dreams at nights: The achingly beautiful blond slave, forced to submit, to adopt the erotic poses demanded of her before the rabble of Rome, or more obsessively, the image came to me as I had first seen her: splendidly tall, naked and chained, her hands clenching the wooden bars of her cage as she looked out with icy disdain on the leering louts who would seek to tame her. And when Lucius spoke of Rome, the reason for my restless discontent came to me in a flash. Thus, the idea began to grow of going to that place, where one might find and personally capture one of those blond beauties. Slowly the idea took shape, and it grew with my unexpected excitement. I must go north!

For someone like me, there was much to recommend such a post. First of all, it was said that with only a few denarii in his purse a man could live like a king among those half-civilized tribes. Then there were rumors, vague but persistent, of hoards of gold kept hidden by the savage chieftains, there for the taking, the rich spoils of the war on the last frontier. It was true that all such booty belonged, in theory, to the emperor, but it was widely known that many an enterprising officer found ways to line his pockets along the way as the spoils of war made their way, not always intact it seems, back to the imperial treasury. And finally there was the legions' generous practice, at some of these more remote locations, of allowing a portion of the captives to be given to the soldiers as personal slaves.

Of course, the choice of any such captives taken in war would first go the officers. That thought inspired me. Did I dare to dream of owning such a woman as that caged, Nordic goddess? Was it so inconceivable that someday I might posses one, or even more of those proud beauties? The thought fired my lust and sent my penis stirring in my loincloth. I became convinced, if indeed I needed any further convincing, that I would request a re-assignment just as soon as I could get back to headquarters.

I knew there were those who would question my judgment, even my sanity, when it became known that I had actually volunteered to be posted to the far frontier. I would request a transfer to Gaul, where troops kept watch along the northern frontier; a place that seemed to many Romans, like the very ends of the earth itself. Everyone knew it to be a land surrounded by dense, gloomy forests, peopled with semi-civilized but unkempt Gauls, savage Saxons, and that fiercely independent Northern tribe known as the Teutons, who lived along the very fringe of the empire. True, these barbarians had been tamed, at least for the moment, but it was widely agreed that renewed fighting might break out at any time. Surely, no sane man would forsake the entice-ments of Rome for so desolate a place! But Lucius had been right. The alluring pleasures of Rome were not for such as us. I swore that when I returned to Rome it would be in tri-umph, as a rich man. Sadly, I came to realize the truth of Lucius' words: The finest delights would always remain the exclusive preserve of the rich and powerful.

Once I had decided my course of action I never looked back, but went straight off to find Flavius, my commander, and then the company's adjutant. Publius looked me up and down, squinting, studying my face with those narrow, brutish eyes of his, highly suspicious as to why anyone should make such an outlandish request. But I stood facing him calmly. With Falvius' written approval in hand, I waited patiently, my expression totally non-committal. He saw that I was determined, and with a shrug and sad shake of his head, he signed the parchment, then stamped it, offi-cially sealing my orders.

Chapter Three

LET THE GAMES BEGIN

And so it was I came to find myself at a place called Bernesium, the only officer in command of the 200-man garrison stationed at a small, but well-built and comfortably solid compound. Our fort stood on a hill, guarding the only approach to the town below. Bernesium was still a garrison town to be sure, the sort of place that inevitably grows up under Roman protection. First came the fort, and then a small colony sent from Rome, and finally the local Gauls had drifted in to cluster beneath the sheltering walls. I was surprised at how large the colony had become. There was even a handful of merchant's and craftsmen's stalls in the marketplace. Peace had been good to this bustling frontier town. At the far end of the town was a large lake with plentiful, tasty fish. The crops were surprisingly lush here, and a brisk trade had grown up as I soon discovered, because the town was at the crossroads of not two, but three, minor trade routes.

Altogether, not such a desolate place after all, I soon

decided. Although that was not at all my impression when I first laid eyes on the place, as my horse slowly crested the top of a gentle hill, and I looked down for the first time on my new home. Spring had not yet come to Gaul, and the landscape was stark, the trees bare. There were little signs of life in the still cold air, though smoke came up from some of the huts. I'll admit that upon first impressions the prospect before me seemed rather bleak, and my first view of the place caused me to I wonder if I'd made a terrible mistake.

By the time spring came that year, however, I had settled in nicely. Bernesium became green and rather pleasant, the air, caressed with soft breezes and the budding fruit trees, promised an early, warm summer. My men were a rough and rather dull lot, but then I hardly expected the spit-and-polish of the Praetorian Guard. On the whole, they were no better, or no worse, than any other company of common soldiers. Fortunately, my sergeant was a competent enough fellow who pretty much ran things, leaving me with considerable leisure time. Somehow Sergeant Metelus managed to take care of things, seeing to the daily affairs of the company, assuring that the men were reasonably satisfied, adequately fed, and paid on time. Bernesium is, after all, a small town, and small towns abound in rumors. I soon heard the rumors concerning the good sergeant: that he had a lucrative side-business, offering extra protection to the local tradesmen whose caravans were constantly coming and going through the wild countryside. I never troubled myself about these matters. After all, we had quickly come to a sort of understanding, one that seemed to work for both of us.

And so, with time on my hands, I set out to explore the

pleasures of Bernesium, and these, for an officer of the legion at least, were to be found in only one place—the house of Gratius. It goes without saying that wherever there are soldiers there will be women and wine, some enterprising entrepreneur will always see to that. As you might expect there were several wine houses in our town clustered around the fort, and even a surprisingly large hostel; but the pleasures of the flesh were provided almost exclusively by one man—Asinus Gratius.

Gratius was an ex-senator, who sensing a shift in the political winds, had hastily and stealthily departed from Rome under rather questionable circumstances. He managed to take with him a considerable fortune, that he used to ease the discomforts of his self-imposed exile by opening a high class house of pleasure at his villa by the lake at Bernesium. Business flourished; the old rogue prospered. I found that Gratius also held the contract with the army to run the women's house next to the barracks. Supplying whores to the army was a lucrative business, and apparently my predecessor had allowed him to set the terms for what turned out to be a generous contract. Along with the written agreement, Sergeant Metelus assured me with a sly wink, was an "understanding" whereby a bit extra might come the way of the garrison commander, "for services rendered"—another arrangement that seemed to me eminently sensible.

Naturally, the common whores who service the troops are seldom visited by the officers, even in remote outposts like ours. Instead, I was invited to avail myself of the more scrumptious treats placed at my disposal at the luxurious villa of the wealthy procurer. A word about Gratius' pride and joy seems in order.

It was on the picturesque lake that the ex-politician chose to build his pleasure palace, recreating a splendid Roman villa in this remote province. Except for the fort, it was the largest compound in Bernesium: A sprawling low building with extended wings that enclosed beautifully manicured grounds surrounding lively fountains and flowing water gardens. A red-tiled roof, and a spacious verandah, set with tall columns in typical Roman style, welcomed the visitor. Inside, the house was exquisitely fur- nished with treasures spirited away on the hasty flight from Rome, along with expensive tapestries, and oriental rugs, that had found their way along the trade routes to our little outpost. In addition to his private rooms, one wing held the women's quarters, where Gratius kept some of finest sex slaves in the province—beautiful, talented young women, whom he made sure were exceptionally well trained.

Gratius' girls were made available to local merchants, visiting traders, and notables like the provincial governor, as well as a few of the town's more important personages, among whom I, as garrison commander, was afforded a very special place. Indeed Gratius saw to it that when vis- iting his house I would be entertained like a king, although only my initial visit was a free one. I remember that visit fondly, the first time I walked along the shady tree-lined paths that meandered down to that idyllic garden of heav- enly delights.

I was met at the door by a wiry little slave girl whose big brown eyes smiled up at me, from under the fringe of an even row of layered bangs. I couldn't help smiling back as my eyes took in her slight girlish shape, the gentle slope of her lithe shoulders and, through a sheer bodice of white silk, the shallow curves of a pair of understated breasts:

small, tautly rounded mounds tipped with surprisingly pert nipples. Brashly uptilted, the little nubbins poked back impertinently against the thin fabric, nosing upward as if hopeful of being petted.

As befits a proper sex slave, the young woman who greeted me was clad in nothing but a Greek-style tunic. Made of white diaphanous silk, this short, sleeveless affair, left bare her supple limbs, the shallow curving neckline being defined by narrow shoulder straps that looped her thin shoulders and exposed a delectable expanse of smooth girlish chest. The thin bodice covered, but did not hide, her maidenly chest, before it fell in soft folds, to be gathered at the waist by a thin belt, thus forming a brief loose skirt— one that barely covered the hips and the top third of her firm, youthful thighs. Open-strapped sandals and a high leather collar (that ubiquitous symbol of her servitude) completed her scanty outfit. The inspiring sight of the slave girl's nubile body as she stood in the doorway, her dusky vulva dimly visible through the milky fabric, brought on a familiar surge of lust, and caused an immediate stirring from under the short kilt of my own tunic.

As I stood there gaping at the girl, this vision of loveliness lowered her eyes, tilted her head in a respectful bow, and politely asked if I would follow her. Then she turned on her heel and led the way down the hall, her small tight behind swaying most delightfully. The little skirt was barely adequate to layer the girl's nicely rounded bottom, so that as she walked the hemline rode rhythmically, threatening to expose more than the undercurves of a cute butt, which peeked out from below the shifting hem with each step. Would I follow her?! Without a doubt, I would have followed that delectable little cupcake to the very gates of Hades itself!

My charming escort led me through the main hall to where my host awaited my arrival in the large circular bay that with its high domed ceiling formed the center of the magnificent house. Gratius was a big, fun-loving bear of a fellow with a roaring laugh and a lusty appetite. He thoroughly enjoyed playing the role of the Province's wealthiest citizen. A life-long bachelor, he was like a jovial uncle to his bevy of slave girls one or two of whom seemed always to be draped about his person.

I came upon him seated like an enthroned monarch on a low-backed camp chair, wearing nothing but a towel draped over his loins, naked thighs spread wide, and sandaled feet planted firmly on the tiled floor. Behind him, a comely lass stood with both hands on his big shoulders, slowly kneading the soft, naked flesh, while on the rug at his feet a second slave girl sat with knees drawn up, her head resting against her master's hairy thigh. One of his hands had dropped down along the side of the chair and the thick fingers were idly playing in the silken mass of the lissome girl's rich, auburn hair.

He greeted me with a friendly wave and beckoned me over to recline on a nearby sofa. Magically, a slave girl appeared at my elbow, instantly ready with a generous cup, and a flagon of fine Latium wine.

"So, Marcus," he began expansively, "how do you find our little corner of the empire? Dull no doubt, after the fun of Rome, eh?"

Eyeing the serving girl who, upon bending down to pour the wine, was at that moment offering me a splendid view of her taut conical breasts as they hung within the billowing neckline of her tunic, I tried to respond to my most magnanimous host as best as I could. Although somewhat distracted, I heard myself assuring him that the present company, at least, was the equal of any to be found in Rome, and he beamed in appreciation of the compliment. It was true, he admitted with a thoughtful nod, that in some ways we had been able to retain "a bit of old Rome" here in the hinterlands. He paused and then, brightened up. For example, there were the games!

"When was the last time you saw a couple of big league gladiators going at it?" he inquired, with a highly amused grin.

I'll admit I was a bit bewildered, but I couldn't help smiling at his obvious enthusiasm. It had been a while, I allowed, remembering those disastrous games where I had lost more than a few denarii betting on the blue team. But there were no games in Bernesium. Surely, my host didn't maintain a stable of gladiators? I soon found that that was not quite the type of contest he had in mind. For after a teasing pause, he enlightened me, grinning broadly, that he had arranged to have a special entertainment staged in my honor. As a man who appreciated the ladies, he leered, he felt sure I would enjoy his very special "gladiators."

Now the master of the house clapped his hands and shouted triumphantly:

"Let the games begin!"

Intrigued, I watched as two hooded figures appeared from between the circle of columns surrounding the room. As they made their way toward us, I saw that they were barefoot, their bodies being covered from neck to ankle in long wine-red cloaks with cowls that turned up to cover their heads. The mysterious figures came to a stop just in front of their seated master where they stood side by side, awaiting his orders.

At an imperious gesture from him, they dramatically threw back their cowls. I found myself staring at two slave girls, young women whose heads were all but shorn, their hair clipped to a short stubble, as was sometimes done to slaves in Rome. They stood at attention, their eyes fixed on some spot over our heads. At a further nod from Gratius, their hands went immediately to the collar of the cloak to open the clasp they found there, and throw back the cloaks from their shoulders. The two garments slithered down to the floor, revealing two naked female bodies, young and taut-muscled, and glistening with a fine sheen of oil. As I watched awestruck, they bowed low in salute to their seated master.

Gratius said not a word but kept them standing there next to one another, knowing that I would want to be able to compare the female wrestlers, for one look at their sheared heads and oil-slicked bodies made it obvious that in that role they would be entertaining us. As Gratius appreciated, in such situations one likes to size up the contestants. And so for a moment we sat in silence, critically evaluating the healthy young females that stood motionless before us. Then Gratius leaned over to me.

"The girl on the left is Leia," he muttered, calling my attention to the rather stocky girl with a full curvaceous body. Her features, like her body had a softly rounded, girlish quality, and one could only guess from the light brown stubble that had been left to her, what she might have looked like with a full head of hair. I next studied her hefty tits. Generous, though not excessive, they drooped slightly to swell into two sloping pendants, crested with wide, thick nipples. Not only was the hair on their head shorn, no doubt useful for wrestlers, but for some more obscure reason, the girls' pubic hair had also been shaved clean. Totally bereft of its natural fuzz, Leia's plump little pubis was pale white and freshly shorn, so that it stood out boldly from between the tanned curves of her powerful thighs.

"And this," my host continued with an expansive gesture, "is Uta." A bit taller than her more muscular rival, Uta had a lean boyish body, slim-hipped; more angular, than curved. Her precisely-made breasts were narrow and pointy, capped with small dusky nipples. Her features were crisp and neat, and with her practically bald head, she had a clean cut look, enhanced by her straight lines, and her denuded sex—a narrow triangle of shiny white flesh tucked between coltish legs. Though she would have been outweighed by her more substantial sister, I saw that she had the hard wiry build of an athlete. She would be a very tough opponent, I surmised.

"Well, what do you think?" Gratius asked at last, breaking my reverie, a note of eagerness creeping into his voice.

"About evenly matched, I should say."

He agreed. Both were strong determined young women, he pointed out. In addition, the girls were intense rivals. It had been his idea to take advantage of their natural rivalry by pairing them off. The winner would be allowed to complete her triumph over her adversary in a very unique way, he assured me with a mysterious wink.

"But come, you must be a betting man?" he asked coyly.

"I would give the edge to Leia," I opined, taking the safer bet.

He smiled. "A modest wager, perhaps?"

I had the sinking feeling that I was being taken, but there seemed no gentlemanly way out. And so I accepted his outstretched hand, and the bet was made.

With a flourish of his hand, Gratius dismissed the wrestlers, who bowed in acknowledgment, and turned to go to take their places on the field of combat. The room we sat in was tiered in three wide levels of descending circles, stepped down so that they led to a sort of sunken circular pit in the middle of the room. Gratius and I were seated on the topmost level. Now the girls turned their backs to us and I watched the rare view they presented as they descended the three board steps that led to the sunken arena. Leia had the more generous ass, roundly plump and voluptuous, while Uta sported a pair of sleek ovals that formed narrow hard-muscled buttocks. In the center circle, a set of mats had been laid. Down-stuffed and covered with hard, smooth linen, they made the ideal surface for a slippery wrestling match, my host assured me proudly.

Now the two naked women separated to stand across the rink from each other, eyeing each other intently, poised and alert, like two gladiators sizing up their opponent for the point of weakness. At a word from their master, they crouched over, and began to warily circle each other.

I watched my champion with keen interest, the sturdy girl with her feet firmly planted in a widened stance. Leia moved slowly, with extreme caution, always sideways, her eyes locked on her opponent, searching for the right opening. Her full breasts fell forward and hung in firm rounded mounds as she instinctively widened her stance and lowered her crouch, scuttling flat-footed and solid, hands extended, the gleaming muscles of her arms and shoulders moving liquidly, as she grimly circled her opponent. Meanwhile Uta, was also moving slowly, her lean body poised like a cobra about to strike. Her slight breasts assumed the shape of narrow, pointy, tit bags, swinging from side to side beneath her bowed torso when she crouched down, and began to move her lowered shoulders with slow menace. My eyes studied her face: the narrowed eyes, and the determined set of her tightly-drawn lips. The girl was ready to spring! Her tense body coiled down tightly, sleek calve muscles straining, as she rose up on her toes and bounded lightly, one hand beckoning, taunting her rival.

But Leia would not be drawn to make the first move, and the two continued to circle till I wondered if they would ever close. Then it happened! Uta with a savage shout, bounded forward with head lowered aimed right at her opponent's belly. Leia reacted just in time to deflect the shorn head, although she took a glancing blow to the body that propelled her backward, so that she staggered and almost lost her balance. But she recovered in a flash and instantly the two women were locked together in a death grip, arms tightly clasped around each other's slippery body, grappling and twisting with wide spread legs, desperately straining to keep their balance.

Leia, managing to get a leg between the other girl's, pressed forward, using her upper body strength to slowly bend the slender girl back under her superior weight. But somehow Uta managed to slip away with a quick slashing move that brought her slithering out of the bear-like grasp. Both girls were finding that getting a purchase on a twisting, writhing, oil-slicked body was obviously a very difficult challenge. Now the action became hot and heavy: the two combatants closed again, spinning and gyrating in a brief but furious blur of limbs. Once again, the embrace could not be sustained and the two obviously excited wrestlers, sweating and panting from their exertions, fell apart once more, to begin once again their slow cautious circling.

I shot a quick glance at my host to find him leaning forward, his eyes keen with excitement. His gaze was riveted on the sweaty scene, fascinated by the slow deadly dance of the fighting femmes. My own excitement was rising at the sight of these naked girls squirming hotly in the heat of combat, and now my need was making itself felt by pressing against the front of my kilt with alarming urgency.

A warrior's yell drew my attention back to the combatants who were struggling strenuously. Uta had somehow managed to get herself behind the other girl and had her arms wrapped around her from the back. As Leia struggled to shake her off, Uta fumbled for a better grip, groping wildly till her clutching fingers closed on a handful of her opponent's oily tit. The fingers tightened, clenching the slick mound of flesh in a fist, causing its owner to cry out in pain, and shake even more furiously to dislodge her attacker. Leia managed to bend forward and reach between her legs to grab the thrust-forward leg of the wiry girl, pulling it to topple her foe, who fell to the mat with a resounding thud.

In a flash Leia was on her, pouncing, pressing the squirming girl down to the mat. For a moment the two oily bodies wriggled together, slippery breasts grinding against slippery breasts, legs intertwined. Suddenly, Uta managed to squirm out from under the pinning weight of the heavier girl, but she didn't press her advantage for she seemed to pause. She appeared to be a little dazed. Perhaps she had the wind knocked out of her, for now she only managed to draw herself up on hands and knees, while her opponent lept up, ready and alert. Before she knew what hit her, Leia fell on her, and draping herself over Uta's crouched form slithered up the oily back to grab hold of the skinny girl's jiggling tits, and pay her in kind for the savage mauling she had received at Uta's hands. Uta threw back her head and clenched her jaws against the pain, as Leia squeezed the soft slippery handfuls of tittie-flesh till they bulged angrily between her clenched fingers.

The rough treatment seemed to enrage Uta, and her desire for revenge must have given her superhuman strength, for she suddenly squirted out from under the draping form of the heavier girl, and it was Leia who spilled down onto the mat, falling flat on her belly. Moving with frantic speed, the wiry girl flipped her opponent over and sat on her, straddling her hips, planting her bare bottom firmly on the Leia's twisting loins. While Leia bucked desperately, Uta took aim and swatted the heaving mounds of Leia's tits, giving three of four vicious slaps to other girl's breasts. Leia was screaming and tossing her head from side to side, as Uta slapped her floppy breasts repeatedly. Then Uta fell forward, covering Leia's nude form with her own well-oiled body; pinning her dazed opponent to the mat. She threw back her head and shouted out a triumphant count of three. Hers was a clear and convincing victory.

Chapter Four

A RECONCILIATION, OF SORTS

The two combatants untangled themselves slowly and managed to struggle to their feet. They turned to face their master, panting heavily, chests heaving. They stood collecting themselves for a moment, bowed deeply, and then straightened up to brace at attention, awaiting their master's pleasure, while their undulating breasts evened out in slow recovery. The two combatants stood flushed and sweating profusely; rivulets of perspiration mingled with the scented oil to form a glistening sheen that coated their exhausted bodies. Leia's quivering bosom still bore the angry red imprints where she had been slapped, but all other traces of anger seemed to have dissipated from both girls, now that the contest was over.

"Ah, yes, to the victor goes the spoils!" Gratius cried, giving me a sly wink. "Come here, Uta, and accept your prize."

But as the girl started forward, he stopped her. "But, wait! We almost forgot. First, you must kiss and make up. Let us all be assured that there are no hard feelings."

The slave girls showed no surprise, but obediently turned

to one another, and opened their arms to accept each other's gleaming body in sisterly embrace. But it was hardly a sisterly kiss that was delivered when Uta kissed Leia, hard, directly on the open mouth. These well-trained slaves knew exactly what their lascivious master desired to see. For a moment, the two young women stood locked in a deep kiss, swaying slightly. Their arms tightened, as their warm bodies fitted together. The kiss broke, and the sweaty girls held each other loosely, looking into each other's eyes.

"Uta, I think perhaps you've hurt your friend. That wasn't very nice, the way you so shamelessly treated her lovely breasts. Now, you must say you're sorry, and kiss them a little, just to make them feel better," my randy host urged, clearly enjoying himself with a devilish gleam in his eye.

The thin girl mumbled an apology, and ducked her head, bringing her lips to the recently-abused tits. The kisses she bestowed were dry and perfunctory—a quick brush on each throbbing mound.

"No, better than that!" Gratius demanded.

Again Uta lowered her head and nuzzled Leia's breasts, while her companion stood stock still, her arms hanging loosely at her sides, letting herself be kissed. As the lips caressed her sensitive tips, Leia let her head fall back while arching up her chest to accept the soothing relief offered to her ample bosom. Now Uta was kissing all over those tautly rounded curves, dragging her tongue after her lips, licking the still-oily tits lavishly, while Leia sighed and closed her eyes. A tiny smile came to her lips as she luxuriated in the waves of pleasure.

"Her nipples—suck on her nipples!" Gratius croaked in voice hoarse with passion.

Leia arched back even further, raising up those choice tips for the loving attention of her rival, while Uta nosed into a soft, elastic mound of flesh, and drew a big, pink nipple in between her teeth. She brought up a hand to cup the bulging tit, holding it firmly as she worked the nipple gently between her lips, drawing on the pliant tip, sucking softly, making Leia squirm in sensual delight. Only when he was satisfied that both nipples had been given adequate attention, did Gratius comment on the game.

Uta kept one arm slung loosely over Leia's shoulder, while Leia slipped an arm around her rival's waist. Gratius smiled at the gesture of sisterly affection. It was now obvious that Uta's ministrations had been successful for the glistening nipples had grown and flowered; the aureoles tautly expanded; protruding tips stiff with excitement.

"Well, Leia, I see that you enjoyed making up. But shouldn't you thank Uta for being so nice to your sore titties? After all, she's the one who *won* the contest. Surely, it's *you* who owes her proper tribute, no?" The lusty rogue was enjoying himself immensely. "Come now. It's time you paid your proper respects to the conqueror. On your knees, my girl!"

Leia obediently slipped free from the loose embrace, and sank to her knees before her rival. Uta smiled down on the other girl in smug triumph, and went to reach for her defeated rival's head.

"No, Uta! Turn around, and show us your cute bottom. Lean well over, and spread your legs."

When she leaned forward to brace herself on her thighs, the bottom in question was offered in lewd invitation to the woman who knelt behind her.

"Go on, Leia! Kiss that perfect little behind of hers!!!

And you better do a thorough job! I want you to show your proper respects. After all, to the victor goes the spoils!" Gratius crowed, highly amused at this display of his own perverted humor.

Leia did not hesitate, but brought her head forward to bring her lips to the jutting ass of her victorious rival. There she planted a long, lingering kiss, before licking and kissing all over the taut curves of those protruding cheeks, while Uta deepened the bow in her back, arched up and wiggled her shoulders in sheer sensual delight, savoring the delicious feel of that obeisant, hard-working tongue.

We watched fascinated, as Leia's gleaming head with its faint stubble, moved in on the proferred ass, so she could thoroughly lap those twin curves. A powerful surge of lust welled up in me to see Leia making love to little Uta's rump. My cock stiffened at the powerfully moving sight.

Once she had that narrow butt covered with a sheen of saliva, the randy whoremaster instructed the kneeling girl to clasp Uta by the hips, and thrust her tongue deep into the other girl's crack. The wet, probing tongue electrified Uta, who shot upright. A shiver of pleasure shot up her spine, rippling through her shoulders, as the slithering tongue insinuated itself deep in her narrow cleft. Getting increasingly agitated, my insatiable host ordered the slavish girl to open up the clamping cheeks so as to expose Uta's tiny anus. She was to pleasure the other woman by applying her tongue to the cringing asshole, and this she would do with wild enthusiasm, for by now both young women were squirming in heat, their excitement reaching a feverish pitch.

Uta had her eyes clenched tight. Her bald head was bobbing rhythmically. I saw her hands tighten on her knees as she held on against the wild thrills being generated by that intimately probing tongue. Leia dug her thumbs into the deep division between those tight cheeks, and pried the pliant mounds apart, licking assiduously, rooting in between the splayed cheeks with enthusiasm, till she had her rival moaning and writhing helplessly.

Suddenly the old satyr, with his perverse sense of timing, abruptly ordered a stop to the action.

Leia fell back to sit on her heels, her shoulders slumped, heaving raggedly. Her head was hung low. Her face was flushed and she was panting through her opened mouth. Uta was summoned to take her place before her lord and master. As she mounted the stairs, the serving girl came to her master's side, holding the prize that had been designated for the victor. I was amused to see that what she held in her hand was a well-formed phallus, long and narrow and fashioned of smooth ivory. The slave girl was busy oiling the shaft, running her curved fingers up and down its length to apply a generous coating of oil. I also noticed that the rod appeared to be set into a sort of harness, from which a set of straps dangled down.

At a nod from the seated monarch, the serving girl proceeded to equip the victor with her award. She assisted as Uta stepped into the leather loops and drew the contraption up her legs, where it was buckled snugly into place around the girl's straight, lithe body. The leg straps were tightened around that tight little butt, while a strap that had been left hanging down in front was now brought between her legs and secured to the back of the belt. Finally, the straps were pulled tight and cinched into place, thus providing the skinny girl with a bobbing phallus that stuck straight out from her vulva in a perverse parody of the male scepter.

Gatitus was pleased. He smiled and beckoned the girl to him so that he might personally inspect the tightness of fit. He ran his fingers along the belt that cinched Uta's waist, and followed the snug leg straps that curved under her boyish butt. He yanked on the center strap, tugging the thin leather strip even deeper so that it was embedded between the girl's labia. Turning her around, he gave her a friendly smack on the bottom that sent her scampering back down to the combat arena. I watched these fascinating preparations, utterly taken by the sight of the slightly-built girl sporting a phallus that bobbed obscenely as she bounded down the stairs to where her rival awaited her.

Uta knew what to do. I got the distinct feeling that this was not the first time that these slave girls had been made to put on such a show before their lecherous lord. Stepping up to the kneeling girl she reached down and paused to fondle Leia's right breast. Leia looked up at her, and when their eyes met, Uta placed a hand flatly at the top of the girl's chest and pushed steadily, shoving her backwards so that the Leia fell onto her back, propped up on her elbows, legs sprawled out on the pillows.

Uta knelt down beside her, the phallus bobbing and swaying as she did so. Gradually, she lowered herself so the two slave girls lay snuggled together side by side on the mat. I expected to see a swift business-like penetration, and perhaps some perfunctory and disinterested fucking, but these girls had been well trained and they knew their master's preference for a Sapphic performance that was slow and loving. And so they embraced and kissed, warmly and tenderly, holding each other and moving together like lovers often do. Their oily bodes were intertwined, the kisses getting longer, deeper as they squirmed hotly on the mat. Heated hands moved up and down each other's body, exploring the slippery curves with increased urgency.

I quickly glanced at my host to see that he had summoned the girl who a sat at his feet. She must have known her master's unspoken wish for this lissome girl proceeded to docilely lay herself down across his lap, draping her slim, supple body over his widespread thighs so that her head hung down at one end, and her legs angled down to the floor at the other.

The casually-assumed pose served to present the slave girl's randy master with her perky, upturned bottom. His hand casually brushed up the little skirt of tunic to uncover that splendid feminine behind: a superb bottom ready to be admired, stroked, and fondled as he watched the sweaty girl-on-girl action unfolding before him. For a moment he paused to consider that shapely little butt, then his hand moved, cupping the tautly-rounded skin at the back of a thigh and following that smooth column till it slid up to capture a pert, neatly-rounded cheek, and there it lingered, lightly squeezing and enjoying the feel of that pleasing curve.

My own need was soaring towards a climax and I rushed to follow my host's example. Pulling the little serving girl to me, I brushed back my kilt, and placed her small oily hand squarely on my swollen penis.

Now the two lovers were writhing in the full bloom of raging passion. Uta was slowly massaging a handful of Leia's ample tit, while the other girl had managed to get a hand between them, and currently had a finger inserted up Uta's vagina. I watched them moving, sliding slickly over one another, till Uta had gained the dominant position, her body placed along the length of her lover's.

Uta reached down to throw open Leia's legs. Suddenly, Leia became strangely passive, letting her slack limbs be rearranged, looking up at her dominating lover with lips parted and expectant. Uta passed a hand between those loose legs and fondled her rival's denuded sex, causing the poor girl to whimper in her desperate need. Then, getting up to kneel between the splayed legs, she reached down to hold the phallic rod, and guide it to the gaping lips of her defeated lover.

Enraptured by the fiery lesbian action, I couldn't take me eyes off the hot performance. When I managed to swallow the sudden upsurge of pleasure and open my eyes again, I saw that the rod had been inserted between Leia's slick lips. Uta drove in, falling forward, plunging the carved phallus right into the churning depths of her lover's sex. She started to move immediately, her hips bucking in smooth even rhythm that had the gleaming shaft pistoning in and out of the hot, clinging cunt. Leia groaned and tossed her head from side to side, being driven mad with pleasure as her sister fucked her with the ivory shaft.

I tried to ignore the hand on my prick, but the exquisite feel of those slim oily fingers wriggling their way over my erect manhood sent me soaring to ecstatic heights, so that I had to fall back weakly on the couch. With a surge of effort I worked to repress the urge to come, struggling against the rising tickle of excruciating pleasure, vowing to hold on a bit longer with all the determination I could muster.

Through half-lidded eyes I saw that the expression on Uta's face matched my own grim determination as she drove in ruthlessly, savagely violating her fellow slave with an intensity that surprised me. She had Leia openly moaning now, thrashing about on the mat, her hips undulating in time to the crashing pounding she was being given. I watched Leia's wide-spread legs begin to slowly rise, instinctively coming up to invite even deeper penetration till her feet were fluttering high in the air, and her thighs were grappling with the other girl's thrusting loins.

Uta bucked furiously, riding her conquest till she came, deriving whatever pleasure she could from seeing the other woman helpless and moaning below her. When she dismounted, leaving her defeated rival in a depleted heap, the insatiable phallus was still sticking straight out from her loins, bouncing eagerly as if looking for new conquests.

At that moment, the little minx who held my manhood loosely in her curled fingers, tightened her little fist, and viciously yanked on me. The sudden stab of pleasure brought my hips high up off the couch and I twisted there in the wind, caught in the tight grip of that little feminine hand. Again and again she jerked, and I came in an explosion of intense pleasure.

You would have thought that Leia's climax might have ended the performance, but the voracious sexual enthusiast who ruled the manor had not yet reached his own satisfaction. He was happily spanking the little ass of the girl who writhed in his lap, shouting his encouragement to Uta all the while, when Leia came with a mighty thud. He paused in his efforts to warm the girlish bottom on his lap. He was pleased, yet not quite ready to dismiss his prized "gladiators." He had one final demand. A thoughtful expression came over his face as his hand slowly rubbed the heated cheeks of the girl who squirmed hotly on his lap. Turn about was fair play, he pontificated in prim tones.

Uta was to unbuckle the contraption and hand it over to

her rival, so that it might be secured around Leia's robust loins. The vanquished would thus be allowed to take her revenge on her conqueror and the next command showed just how fiendish that lovable old satyr really was. It was her master's desire that the phallus be used as a back-door weapon. She would be instructed to savage the other girl's skinny ass—an order she carried out with considerable gusto.

Chapter Five

CURIOUS PLEASURES

Among the unique delights of the House of Gratius were the many novel and imaginative ways devised by the inventive proprietor to display his girls for the perusal of his many guests and customers. I well remember the day when the pretty slave who met me at the door escorted me straight through the big house to where my host waited for me on the back verandah. This porch was built as a wide curve, a semi-circle that jutted out, opening onto the grassy lawn below and giving a superb view of the lake. A line of tall columns was set along the outside rim of the sweeping verandah.

And now I saw that to each column our ingenious host had affixed a female slave! Each girl was secured with her hands against her side, her back to the column, and kept in place by three thin leather strips that looped her nude body: one cutting into the soft flesh just below the breasts; another snugly belting her loins by spanning her hips; the third pressing tightly into the flesh across at line at mid thigh. On a leisurely summer's day one could stroll along the verandah, enjoying the view, pausing here and there to admire these "living statues" that adorned the vista, perhaps to run one's hands over a firm young body, or to sample between one's fingers a conveniently-placed nipple.

Guests were encouraged to handle the wares. And sometimes games and contests were held, each more perversely erotic than the last. One of the favorite games of the male guests (and the occasional female guest as well) would involve arousing the slave girls' passions, fondling their healthy, responsive bodies shamelessly till they had the young women squirming in the heat of desire. The object was to see who would be the first to bring his "statue" to a climax. For this game the slaves were blindfolded, and then tied in such a way that their legs were stretched open and held apart, giving free access to their splayed pussies. Gratius, who had thoroughly explored the many uses of olive oil, would see to it that a generous coating of that versatile lubricant would be poured over the tightly-bound slaves, so that their lustrous bodies stood gleaming in the sunshine.

Quite naturally, I had the opportunity to try my hand at this contest, selecting a slightly built girl whose dimly circumscribed breasts sported plump little nipples that stuck out impudently, just begging to be touched. I came up to her now, as my fellow contestants (there were four of us) took their respective places along the curving line of columns.

I stood only inches from the slave, admiring her short, close cropped hair. Most of her features were hidden by the wide silk swath that formed the blindfold, but I could tell that she was fair of skin; her hair, a soft golden brown; her neatly-chiseled lips, pursed and full of promise. The slave girl stood alertly, small pointed chin held high above the collar that banded her throat, lips expectantly parted, her young, hard body keen with anticipation. My eyes took in her splayed out form, the vulnerable womanhood pulled open between the sinewy muscles of those out-stretched thighs, the trim ankles, and narrow, delicate feet. I watched her shallow breathing: the lithe, nubile chest gleaming with oil; the slight swells of her young nascent breasts glistening, pert nipples shining in the noonday sun.

When I put my hands around the girl's banded neck she flinched, drawing in a sharp gasp of surprise at the first contact, for I had approached her stealthily, and the blindfolded young woman didn't know that a silent admirer stood watching her only inches away. I moved my hands up her neck to hold her face between my hands. Still holding her, I drew one finger across her small mouth, pressing the fleshy lips back. This charming creature obediently opened her mouth to readily take in my impertinent finger, and begin sucking on it. The girl was superbly well trained! I moved my finger in her hot little mouth exploring the palpitating tongue, tracing the gums, the ridge of teeth, while she sucked and moved her lively tongue under and around my probing digit. Extracting my finger, I slid my hands over the collar and down her neck, to rest them on the girl's oily shoulders.

Now I let my hands appreciate the subtle contours of that fine lustrous body, moving down and up the lines of her supple arms while her small hands clenched in mounting excitement. Clasping the knobs of her shoulders, I flattened my palms and brought my hands together at the top of the girlish chest. Then I slowly drew my hands down, over the faint ridge of the collarbone, sliding over the slick skin onto the soft rises of her maidenly tits, pressing the heels of my palms into those pliant swells, no more than slightly raised disks, with exact centers delineated by those impertinent nipples. The girl stiffened and held herself rigidly still as I pressed my palms into the yielding softness of her small, pancake tits.

Slowly, I brought my hands down till my fingertips felt the pebbly-hard nipples. I moved my palms pressing them into the surrounding softness; moving them in tiny circles. The responsive little slave curled her lower lip and bit down with a row of tiny white teeth, trying to stifle the whimper that managed to escape as I palmed her sensate nipples in a small, circular massage. It didn't take much of this till I had the healthy young girl moving her shoulders, squirming with the rising heat.

Excited by watching her growing arousal, I gently plucked at the stiffening buds, pinching the slippery nipples between thumb and forefinger, rolling the little nubbins as I tugged on the elastic flesh, pulling to stretch her pliant nipples till she groaned under the sweet torture. I soon had those tips swollen with excitement, the aureole expanded, tiny stems protruding saucily. The girl tried to arch back against the pillar, raising her bosom, silently begging to offer me even more, but I had other territory to explore. And so I left those pretty tits heaving in ragged undulations, their excited tips throbbing and proudly erect, and I moved on, sliding my palms along their shallow under curves and down her slippery body, over the traces of the ribcage and beyond, down her taut belly. The slave girl sighed: a sigh of disappointment, or perhaps a sigh of relief, I couldn't tell which.

Now my hungry hands glided along the tightly drawn skin of her belly, moving back and forth between the ridges of the jutting hipbones, delighting in the smooth feel of that satiny skin. My fingers were soon edging along the light haze of fuzz, darkened with oil, that started low on her belly and trailed down to form the thicket of moist curls spreading over her splayed under arch. Crouching down before her, I visually inspected, but did not yet touch, the girl's vulnerable pussy. Instead, I placed my hands on her hips and slowly followed the flaring contours of her haunches over the cradle of her hips and down onto her tapering thighs. I traced along the straining thigh muscles. The tendons stood out, sculpting and shaping the sinewy contours so that I could follow the resulting plane that sloped into the silken flesh of the inner thigh. I ran my fingers up and down her inner thighs, edging always closer to the center of her arch. I saw the tautly drawn tendons twitch, as I stroked her young thighs.

A demanding surge of lust shot through me, and I abruptly got to my feet. Stepping close to the bound girl, only inches from her taut body, I pressed down along her belly with the heel of my hand and was soon palming the slave girl's pubic mound, rubbing it, gently at first, then more firmly fondling that fleshy Mound of Venus while the girl leaned back and let her jaw drop. And from her open mouth came a soft, shivering moan.

I held the girl by her sex and closed my hand, cupping the arch of her pubic bone, curling my fingers up into the soft folds of flesh between her legs, squeezing the bulging lips of her vulva, feeling her incredible inner heat. My fingers felt along her protruding nether lips, pressing in, the middle one slipping into the delicate folds to probe her slick depths and getting a shuddering moan of pleasure. As my finger slid wetly all the way up into her cunt, the girl gave out with a long low groan from somewhere deep in her throat.

I watched her blindfolded face, saw the twinge of urgency crease her brow; saw her twitch, squirming helplessly, her hips moving sensually against the pillar. Arching back, she rolled her head from side to side as I jiggled the finger, now buried to the hilt in her slick, little vagina. She strained back, raising her hips and grinding her hot sex against my palm while the tendons of her thighs grew rigid, the muscles tightening as she thrust upward. The erotic sight of the lusty young girl, burning with sexual heat, sent my pulse racing, a thrill of desire surging up in me, driving me to take her. To hell with the contest!

Tingling with excitement, I tore at my clothes, snatching off tunic and loincloth, till I stood in nothing but my sandals, my turgid penis proudly standing up in bold salute to the naked young woman sensually writhing before me. Positioning myself right between her archate legs, I guided my straining penis to the edge of the gaping pussy and abruptly took her, lunging forward, driving up her wet, pulsating vagina in a single powerful thrust that caused the girl to stiffen and draw in a sharp hiss of breath through clenched teeth. I clamped her slick hips, and holding on to her with both hands, wiggled my loins while thrusting upward, burying my engorged prick up her cunt to the hilt. The impaled female threw back her head; let out a low, earthy moan of deep, rutting satisfaction.

The heavenly feel of that tight young pussy was exquisite and I fucked the girl with deep full strokes, pumping into her, speeding up till I was bucking my hips with furious abandon, crazed by lust to see the slave girl's hot, twisting body thrashing about in erotic frenzy. She was making tiny little grunts now with each thrust of my loins, a crisp staccato that told me the girl was getting close to the edge; I held on, grimly determined to match my release to hers. I felt the tremendous upsurge of my climax, and rammed into her, holding myself in place, buried in her churning depths, as she gasped and stiffened. She cried out in a long, lingering moan, as a tremor rippled through her thin frame, followed by a more definite shudder—deeper and more massive. I came in an thunderous explosion of pure pleasure while the slave girl shook and trembled in the throes of orgasmic delight, and then went limp, sagging in her bonds.

After the contest the depleted girls were released and allowed a few moments to rest and collect themselves, before being sent to the lake to wash off all traces of oil, and whatever other fluids might be decorating their bodies. They followed this routine with enthusiasm, racing down to the edge of the water, plunging in from the outcrop of rock, swimming and cavorting in the shallow lake, their close cropped hair wetly plastered down, those hard, young bodies glistening with sheens of streaming water as they climbed out onto the rocks. To see the bevy of nude beauties shrieking and frolicking in the lake like spirited water nymphs, was truly invigorating, and already my recovering manhood was raising its head in a definite renewal of interest. I don't know who first started toward the inviting lake, but all of a sudden the handful of naked male guests were running pell-mell in a mad rush to join the girls. Soon we were joyfully splashing and swimming among them, making mock attacks and being attacked in turn as small feminine hands found our vulnerable parts, exciting us with slithering underwater caresses.

⸺ ◦◦◦ ⸺

Over the next several months I got to know Gratius quite well, becoming a regular guest at his frequent orgies. He was a man who partook fully of the joys of life, wallowing in lust, and shamelessly indulging his unflagging passion. Now I have observed that every man has some secret obsession, some particularly perverse whim, that were he able to freely indulge, would send him to unimagined heights of the sheerest ecstasy. Gratius was no exception.

Almost twenty years older than me, he had a wealth of experience in a lifetime devoted to the decadent pursuit of pleasure. But even though he may be slightly jaded in the ways of the flesh, Gratius still found youthful delight in one aspect of the feminine anatomy. He was totally enamored with the well-made female posterior! Gratius was a man who absolutely adored a shapely bottom, and he maintained that there were few pleasures greater than that derived from merrily spanking a choice, well-placed rearend. Enthusiast that he was, he had raised spanking to an art form. It was a sport I had tried once or twice in Rome, but never fully appreciated till I learned the finer points at the hands of Gratius of Bernesium.

I had seen him take the occasional playful swat at the tail of a passing slave girl as she was sent scampering off to do his bidding. And of course I had noticed that he was happily engaged in spanking the little slave who had positioned herself over his lap during the memorable fight of the well-oiled "gladiators." But on that occasion I had been much too preoccupied myself to pay a great deal of attention to my host. It was not really until one day in the baths when I saw the maniacal gleam in his eye as he walloped a bouncing ass, that I realized the intense pleasure the act of spanking gave the man.

Among the many Roman customs Gratius had transplanted to his provincial villa, were the pleasures of the bath. A true Roman, he strongly believed in cleanliness, insisting that his girls bathe daily. And of course he loved to join them. It was there that I sometimes found him, and on one occasion as we sat in the warm languorous air, naked, being attended to by a handful of female slaves in the short, hip-length tunics that were the livery of the House of Gratius. In the thick, steamy, perfumed air, the flimsy tunics had become damply transparent, and the wet fabric clung to every contour of their hard young bodies. We had had a few cups of wine and Gratius had grown expansive. I said little, only nodding now and then, while he went on, waxing philosophical. His monologue was on one of this favorite subjects—the pleasures of the flesh.

As he rambled on, I kept one eye on the fetchingly-clad slaves, especially a splendid, tall girl, lean and long-limbed, with raven black hair that fell to her shoulders, and a pair of the most startling blue eyes. She noticed my attention, and lowered her eyes, smiling slightly, as though not displeased at all by my obvious interest. By now I was intimately familiar with all of Gratius' slaves, but I had never seen this one before, for surely I would have remembered her.

Gratius, not for the first time, was rhapsodizing on his favorite sport, the delightful spanking of a bounding female bottom, all the while idly watching the little slave, whom I had last seen upended over his lap. This was Rea, one of his favorites, and she was presently in the act of gathering up some towels. As she bent down, the tunic skirt slid up to lay wetly plastered over the top third of her largely exposed buttocks. The gesture was enough to stop my host in mid-sentence. A sharp word of command caused the girl to freeze as she was, her trim rearend half turned in our direction. "It is the irresistible allure of a well-made bottom, that appeals so invitingly to the hand," he explained, his gaze fixated on the elegant curve of the girl's haunches, the seductive roundness of those jutting twin mounds. "To experience the fullest pleasure," the lecherous connoisseur continued, "one must learn to absolutely savor the moment." So saying, he invited the bending Rea to his lap. He would be glad to show me how it should be properly done, should I care to see a demonstration. I might even want to practice myself on one of the handy slaves, he continued; perhaps the new girl, Maya, he allowed, noting the obvious interest I had in the tall dark-haired slave.

Soon we were both seated with knees widespread on separate benches placed across from one another, with a slave girl sprawled over each lap. The raven-haired girl came to lay over my spread thighs so that her inverted head dangled down over my left leg her long hair falling to the floor, while her extended legs angled down, till her toes touched the floor on the right. I felt her weight on my bare thighs, the press of a hip that rested solidly up against my upstanding phallus.

Gratius began by running his curved hand up and down the back of the girl's bare legs; I followed suit, enjoying the smooth feel of those long tapering thighs, while Maya wiggled to get more comfortable. I watched him slip his hand up higher to ride up onto the little skirt and slowly rub the slippery fabric over the taut mounds, all the while brooding on the brevity of man's life. Then the randy philosopher slid the slippery fabric up and over the twin slopes, baring Rea's small neat bottom to his insatiable eyes. I thrilled at the pleasant prospect of unveiling the lovely swells of Maya's upturned bottom. Firmly cupping a handsome cheek through the slick silk, I gave her a reassuring squeeze. I smiled to see her little cheeks instinctively clench, as I felt up her taut-skinned, hardened butt.

I spent several minutes squeezing and massaging that charming buttocks through the wispy damp fabric, watching them clench and slacken, savoring the delicious feel, the inner softness of those firm, young mounds, admiring the perfect symmetry of those lovely, twin curves that seemed to quiver under my hand. With delicate precision, I pinched the gauzy film away from her hips and worked it up, holding it between thumb and forefinger, exposing a nicely-poised bottom; the twin curves smooth and sleek and divided by a tight crack. The fig of the girl's pursed vulva, adorned with wispy tufts of black pubic hair, peeked out saucily from between her loose thighs. The sight of her half-hidden pussy send a surge of shimmering excitement racing through me and I couldn't resist bringing a finger up to lightly touch her, just there, getting a reflexive twitch of the hips as the girl wiggled and shifted uneasily in my lap.

These were the preliminaries which Gratius assured me were of the utmost importance, the toying foreplay, so necessary to assure that the smoldering excitement would build in both the seated master, and the laid-out slave. And so I spent some time leisurely playing with the slave girl's naked rump, letting my host set the pace. I watched as he slid his flattened hand up to rest it firmly on the small of Rea's back, pinning her in place and I did likewise, spreading my knees to better balance the long-bodied girl's languid weight, placing a hand on her back to steady her. I saw Maya's butt muscles clench tight as the fearful slave girl tensed up in anticipation, the sleek sides of her cheeks hollowing out, the dark arroyo squeezed to a narrow slit. She steeled herself in anticipation of what she knew was about to come!

Together, my host and I both raised our right hands, and at his nod, we both struck.

WHAP! WHAP! two shots rang out almost simultaneously and the two girls bounded up, kicking their heels and yelping in startled reflex. Before she had time to recover, I slapped again, whacking Maya's bottom with crisp authority, using the flat of my hand to deliver a glancing blow that sent her jelly-like mounds juddering. I heard the girl cry out; her legs swinging up behind, scissoring the air frantically. Merrily, I smacked that bounding bottom again and again, relishing the bouncy resiliency of young Maya's wobbling rear cheeks.

The girl jerked forward with each impact, her legs kicking wildly now, while she twisted and squirmed across my lap. I immediately clamped my left hand down even harder on the small of her back, pinning her in place solidly across my open thighs while I spanked her soundly, thoroughly enjoying the sight of her quivering mounds, as they danced under my repeated slaps.

I walloped the trembling swells with grim determination, watching them heave and redden under the unrelenting assault. The black-haired girl was yelping now,

– 58 –

each sharp cry punctuated by the resounding echo of a crisp slap as I mercilessly smacked the quivering, blushing bottom. For a while she tried to deflect the blows by twisting her hips, and when that didn't work she tried to steel herself by tightening her cowering cheeks in anticipation. But under my steady smacking she soon realized the futility of trying to resist and, in time, she simply went limp, allowing her butt muscles to slacken, yielding to the continual assault, accepting her spanking like a good girl, with passive resignation.

After several exciting minutes spent walloping the slave girl' s tight-cheeked, young bottom, my hand was tingling, throbbing with a dull ache, which forced me to stop and rest. I used the pause to admire my handiwork. The flushed cheeks of Maya's handsome bottom were throbbing with a rosy hue. I couldn't resist feeling up that well-spanked behind, savoring the pleasant warmth I had generated in her burning rearend. A plaintive whimper came from the inverted head of my long-legged slave girl, and she squirmed her hips in sensual delight, signaling to me that the heat she was feeling as a result of the spanking was not confined to her well-warmed ass.

Chapter Six

A Day at the Races

As the reader might well imagine from the preceding passages, my first summer at Bernesium was not altogether unpleasant. I spent many a leisurely day whiling away my hours there while enjoying the many delights of the house of Gratius. My official duties were hardly burdensome, although we were being increasingly called upon to provide additional patrols, to escort the passing caravans of slavers. It seems that a particularly nasty little war had erupted with the pesky Scythians, closing the normal trade routes so that the slavers were forced to divert their caravans through the mountains and past Bernesium. As a result, slave caravans began arriving in town, sometimes as many as two or three a week. The slavers would set up camp on a grassy plain just on the edge of town. They would have arrived weary after the grueling march through the mountains, content to spend a few days resting and refreshing themselves, and their charges.

The arrival of a fresh batch of slaves was always an

occasion of excitement for the town, for while their masters rested, the training of the slaves continued unabated, and this provided a fascinating show indeed! A crowd of town's people would gather on those warm summer afternoons to eagerly watch the slaves being exercised, sweating and straining as they were put through their paces, under the firm hand of their stern, slave drivers. This interest was especially high if the lot were being trained as sex slaves, as was the case whenever the caravans of Kimar came to town, for this worthy always had the prettiest slaves; inevitably exercised wearing nothing but their high collars, and the wide leather straps that banded wrists and ankles.

The training began early, and was continuous throughout the march. There were many things the young women must learn in order to be able to serve properly. They must learn to be obedient, to readily meet any need that might be placed on them. They must learn the sort of etiquette, posture, and deportment expected of a well-trained slave. They must be taught to adopt the proper pose for presentation: to stand at attention with hands behind their necks; to kneel in servile offering. They must be taught to walk properly, and to step lively. I often saw girls being put through their paces, forced to run in circles, knees raised high, heads thrown back, chin held high, as they raced around the arena, breasts juddering and bouncing freely, much to the delight of the avid onlookers.

Races were run, and various contests staged, wherein the girls were said to learn the importance of discipline and teamwork, though I suspected that the real reason for such games had more to do with the amusement of the slave drivers. I often stopped to watch these games, especially the "chariot races" that were staged with slave girls harnessed to the traces in teams. Of course, these were not the heavy war chariots such as one found in the legions, but specially made lightweight traps, nothing more than a minimal frame of saplings with two spoked wheels attached.

Teams of four, or six girls, were placed on hands and knees; harness straps laid upon their shoulders, and belted to their hard, young bodies. The chariot's traces were then attached to the harnesses along their flanks. Smooth dowels of soft wood were placed between the teeth to serve as bits, so that reins could be attached by which to steer. Since the onlookers were eager to bet on the winners of these contests, one team was designated the "red" team; the other, the "blue." The team's colors were displayed by "tails" provided by the helpful slave drivers. These were plumes made of horsehair, dyed in vibrant color, and sprouting from squat plugs at one end. The plug was oiled, and inserted into a girl's anus; the plume allowed to flop down over her bare bottom. These "tails" form a most amusing and delightful touch.

The team was now ready for the start of the race. But first, the drivers had to be chosen. For this task younger, sprightly, wiry girls were preferred. The drivers were given light switches, which they used with considerable enthusiasm, because the losers, drivers as well as teams, faced inevitable punishment once the race was over. So a simple flick of the light whip was all that was needed to get them going, sending the naked slave girls scrambling over the grass, hips shifting and buttocks churning merrily, as they crawled as fast as they could on hands on knees, pulling the little chariot behind them, while the crowd cheered on its favorites.

After the last of the day's races there was punishment to

be meted out, an event that had the crowd jostling forward, and scrambling to find a place with a good view of the proceedings. The losers were lined up in a row, side by side, with enough distance separating them so they might widen their stance. As one of the slave drivers took his place behind the line, a wicked paddle in his hands, each girl in turn was made to spread her legs, bend down, and clasp her ankles. With well-trained slaves, the punishment proceeded like clockwork. The first girl obediently assumed the position: leaning over, bending from the waist to reach down, and grab her ankles. A single resounding SMACK! rang out as the leather paddle met the jutting bottom, sending the girl jerking in recoil. At the sound of the solid whack, the next girl was to immediately assume the position, promptly offering up her tight young bottom for similar consideration.

Thus, the grim overseer worked his way down the line. And it was woe to the girl who failed to hold the position, for if the recoil should drive her to release her ankles and bound upward, hands flying back instinctively to rub away the hurt (as sometimes happened, particularly with novices), then she would be in for five more. Should the breech of protocol persist, the miscreant would be tied in place over a trestle to receive further punishment in such a way as to assure perfect compliance.

———— ◦∞∞◦ ————

As commander of the local garrison, I was, of course, made most welcome in the slaver's camp. I quickly learned to allow Sergeant Metelus to negotiate with the slavers to arrange for an escort, while I took advantage of their, often lavish, hospitality. No man was more generous with his hospitality than Kimar, a prosperous slave dealer well-known in certain circles in Rome who specialized in providing the very finest sex slaves. It was when I first met him that I first discovered how the more well-to-do slave dealers traveled in the greatest luxury.

I remember my surprise when Kimar, hatched-faced with a perpetual lean and hungry look, first welcomed me to his spacious, and pleasantly cool, tent. Expensive Persian rugs had been thrown down on the grass floor of the tent, silken pillows were strewn about, and couches arranged around low tables heaped with fine food on golden plates so that one might wine and dine in comfort, all the while allowing one's eyes the pleasure of visually caressing the naked bodies of a brace of attractive females. Slave girls were regularly summoned to enchance the surroundings, for Kimar dearly loved to show off his wares. And he did so in a most astonishing ways!

For example, there was the amazing sight that greeted me as I first passed through the folds to enter the dimly lit chamber. There, hanging by her wrists from a rope that ran over a pulley set at the very the top of the high tent post, was a naked woman. She was tall and slender with long dark hair free to spill down over her shoulders. She had been gagged with a strip of red silk, and the rope which held her wrists high over her head had been pulled taut till her sleek curves were stretched out in elongated sinuous lines.

The demanding pose might have quickly become painful had she not been strung up in such a way that her straining toes could just barely touch the rug, thus relieving some of the weight from her arms. A more demanding pose, my host confided, would have the girl trussed up with one leg raised, bent at the knee, the foot tied behind. This would have forced her to balance her weight on one foot only, poised on the very tips of her toes. He seldom used that particular pose, although it had its uses, he assured me with a cryptic smile.

I remember how, on one occasion, the inventive slaver had a girl hanging from the ceiling in a most unusual way. She was a small-breasted girl, built like a gymnast with a reedy, spry body, compact hips, and slim thighs. She had been suspended as "punishment" for some minor offense and, as was often the case, her master decreed that her punishment should serve as entertainment for his guests.

It so happened that I arrived just in time to see her being trussed up. She had been laid on the center of the rug on her belly, her legs pulled apart, arms pulled straight up over her head and wrists bound together. The ropes that hung from pulleys placed at each corner of the tent's ceiling were attached to the ankle and wrist bands, and the lines were tightened hoisting her up till her body hung swaying a few feet off the floor, her lithe torso bowed in shallow curve, legs held open and pulled back, small tits hanging down, and ass upturned, and placed conveniently at hand.

Her master was not quite satisfied with the arrangements. As an additional refinement, he ordered that her slumping head be raised and the long caramel-colored hair pulled back and the hank of hair looped with a cord that was in turn attached to a thin belt that encircled the girl's waist and pulled taut. The effect was to keep her head well up so the poor girl couldn't help but see the guests who came to admire her, and they in turn could watch her eyes as they greedily savored her healthy, young body. Finally, she was gagged, a wadded rag stuffed in her mouth and held in place by a silk scarf wrapped around her head. The gag would stifle any cries that might emerge as her tautly-curved body was freely and lavishly fondled by her master's randy guests.

For the esteemed visitor to Kimar's tent was always graciously invited to sample his wares. There were several of us in the tent that day, and we each politely took our turns slowly passing our hands over the taut curves of that youthful swaying body, cupping the little hanging titties, running a flattened palm down over the shallow curve of the torso, pressing along the slope of the midriff, the under curve of the belly, and on up between the splayed, sinewy legs, to fondle the slightly gaping vagina. The pert, upturned ass beckoned most seductively, simply inviting the masculine hand to feel the small, taut mounds, to squeeze and manipulate those firm little cheeks freely, till the girl shook, and we heard her stifled moans escaping from around the gag.

One fellow stood between the outstretched legs and took advantage of the gaping pussy placed before him, to slide a finger or two between the pinkish lips of the vulnerable vagina. He tickled her innards, diddling the suspended cunt with short tiny thrusts, till the gurgling moans rose in intensity, and he had the girl whimpering in short plaintive cries. Then he pulled back, waiting while she tried desperately to close her needy thighs on his hand. And he teased her like that, toying with her highly responsive body till finally he took pity on the poor girl, and decided to finish her off. We watched him finger fuck the suspended girl with short furious strokes that had her mewing urgent cries, and thrashing about in her bondage.

Kimar always personally accompanied his large slave trains on their journeys to Rome, and when he traveled, he traveled in style. For each journey, he would personally select a handful of the finest women as his private harem for the length of the trip. He had a discerning eye, and the female slaves quickly learned to vie for his attention.

Everyone knew that being chosen by the slave master meant a welcome respite from the long hours of marching; the fortunate women chosen for his personal use, to ease the rigors of the journey, were most magnanimously allowed to ride on the wagons. They were well fed, and well treated. Because their master insisted on cleanliness, they were given the opportunity to bathe frequently. And though they, like the other slaves, were kept naked when in camp, they were allowed to be groomed, and to partake of cosmetics and scents that might serve to increase their appeal to their master. It was these slaves that were so generously shared with local dignitaries, who were given special invitations to visit Kimar's tents.

Once we were ensconced on the couches, and equipped with cups of wine, a handful of these attractive young girls would appear at the entrance to the tent, pleasingly naked, same for the bands of leather at the neck, wrists and ankles. Silently, and without a word from their master, they would enter and immediately arrange themselves shoulder to shoulder, standing in a row before the reclining guests. One could hardly help comparing the bare bosoms thus displayed, breasts of all shapes and sizes to be offered up in comparison that was endlessly and inexplicably fascinating. And then there were the many variations among the furry vulvas tucked between their firm young thighs, all presented by the unabashedly naked slaves in this open show of feminine charms. After a moment or two, the well-trained slaves girls would drop to their knees and bow down, salaaming with their foreheads pressed to the rug in the eastern manner, as they had been taught.

Continuing the routine they had been taught, they automatically rose to their feet, turned around in place, presenting their backs to us, and knelt once more to press their foreheads to the rug a second time, this time offering up their tempting naked butts to the assembled guests. They would hold the subservient pose until released. And sometimes their master made them hold it for a long time indeed, while the guests nibbled at their food, sipped their wine, and made casual conversation. In time, the girls were released, and the guests allowed to pick their companions for the evening in sort of lottery; two slave girls being normally assigned to see to the needs of each male guest.

Increasingly, I was being invited to visit the tent of Kimar, only to find that I was his only guest. As always, he was gracious and most generous, but I couldn't help getting the feeling that he was evaluating me, sizing me up as it were, as though he wanted something from me. In some ways the slaver and I were kindred souls. We shared an endless fascination with the joys of the flesh. Clearly pleased, he would acknowledge with a frank smile of understanding, my genuine compliments of his ability as a true connoisseur of the well-made feminine form. During one of those conversation I had expressed my soulful desire for a Nordic woman, and we found that this, too, was a passion we both shared, though for different reasons.

On this particular night Kimar seemed to be getting closer to something that had obviously been on his mind. He told me how he had always found me a most reasonable man, a man of the world. I waited expectantly. Then it came. Since we both appreciated those rare Northern beauties, perhaps some arrangements might be made to our mutual benefit?

Of course I had heard the rumors of war with the tribes on the frontier? he asked casually. I nodded not wishing to appear ignorant in matters of military intelligence. It was common knowledge that the crafty old slaver had many spies, and I listened most intently to what he had to say on the subject. Should hostilities once again break out with the Tuetons, he went on, we might both profit. He then proposed that I might make special efforts to see that our raids yielded as many of those choice beauties as possible. Moreover, I would then hold these captive women for Kimar, dealing with him exclusively.

Now in those days it was quite common practice for enemy captives to be turned over to interested slavers, who waited like vultures, on the edge of the war zone, instantly appearing after a raid to surround the camp, until they were given the opportunity to bid for the lot. The proceeds of these sales would to go to the treasury in Rome, and it was well-known, though not officially sanctioned, that sometimes a few denarii would find their way into the purse of the commander of the legion. But what Kimar was proposing was that certain captives be withheld from the open auction till the next time his caravan came to town. For each of these exceptional blonde beauties that might be turned over to him exclusively, a handsome sum would be reserved for me—a sort of commission. He called it a "finder's fee."

Of course I saw the wisdom in what he proposed immediately, and I gladly gave him my hand on it. The deal was struck. Smiling broadly over his exclusive triumph, Kimar then announced that now he had a very special treat for me. In honor of our pact, he had reserved an exceptional pair of slave girls just for me.

At the clap of his hands, the two young women appeared, presenting themselves before me, standing side by side. They might have been sisters. These two had the pleasing good looks of certain Gaullic women, and both had similar soft brown hair, the long straight strands worn pulled back from the face, then bound together with a leather thong so that the excess fell in a length that was long and silky like a horse's tail. It was the style much favored among the Gauls. While they were rather young, one looked quite definitely the other's junior. The more youthful of the two had a lean, almost pubescent body with small crescent tits, and a thin haze of down on her slight Venus mound; her companion had the nicely-proportioned body of an attractive, mature woman. She was well endowed with generous breasts, full mounded with just the slightest bit of sag to them, and a plump, thickly-furred vulva. This was Sylla, Kimar said pointing to the older one; the younger girl was named Tomi. They were given to me for the night.

On being presented, the pair instantly assumed the subservient position on their knees, and bowed low. Then they got up and turned to repeat the ritual, offering for my edification, their naked bottoms: the full rounded fleshy buttocks, next to the pert set of rearcheeks. Summoning a couple of slaves to attend to him, my host then settled back. With his business being so satisfactorily concluded, he was now prepared to enjoy a bit of leisure. As for me, I bade the kneeling women rise, and ordered them to attend to me, allowing them to remove my uniform while I stood there motionless, and let myself be undressed. Once naked, I invited my two attendants to join me on the couch. Then I set about exploring their considerable Gaullic charms.

I found myself pressed between the warmth of two delicious, scented, female bodies as we twisted and squirmed together on the couch. I lay rubbing myself all over the Tomi's nubile body, while Sylla's bountiful bosom burned into my back, all soft and warm and lovely. Things were heating up and rapidly threatening to get out of control, when I broke apart to pause so as to prolong my pleasure as much as possible. I swung my legs down to sit on the edge of the couch, my prick rigidly upright, and throbbing with lust, between my hairy thighs. I went to reach for my cup, but Tomi, wishing to please, reached for it at the same time and somehow managed to splash wine down my lap.

For a moment she froze, horrified at what she had done! Had she displeased her master, and would he order that she now be punished for her clumsiness? But I was not *that* kind of master, and besides the girl could easily make amends by licking the up the spilt wine. I had her kneel before me, and merely pointed to my wet thighs. Obediently, her little tongue peeked out from between her small, pursed lips and started licking. Sylla, meanwhile hovered behind me, kneeling on the couch at my back. Now she threw her arms around me, and pressed her body to mine, sensually squirming, grinding her firmly-mounded tits into my back. My eyes slid closed, and I sighed to savor the heavenly feeling of those twin delights.

Meanwhile, Tomi's silken tongue was sliding wetly over my thighs, licking along the contours, delving down between them to get at the soaked pubic hair. I eased my thighs apart, spreading my knees and easing forward to give the slave girl greater access so she could get to my hanging balls. The flutter of her slavish tongue as it licked all over my furry scrotum sent a wild thrill racing though me. Then she was licking at the root of my shaft, sucking up the wine from the spongy pubic hair, before slowly lapping her way up the quivering length of my rigid penis. The feeling of that slow traveling, wet tongue was absolutely exquisite. Having arrived at the crown of my stolid prick, she leaned forward prepared to take me in her mouth, for that was what she thought I desired of her. But at that point I reached down to grab her by the hair and stop the sweet torture of those wet lips, and that devilish tongue.

"No, just *lick*! Lick it all up . . . every drop," I managed to get out in a voice choked with passion.

And as the girl bent her head to follow my injunction, I got a sudden burst of inspiration. Reaching for Sylla, I pulled her around to kneel beside me. Picking up the still half-filled cup, I splashed the remainder of the wine right on her well-endowed chest. She gave a girlish giggle, and shook her shoulders in surprise as the wine trickled down the slopes of her wobbly tits. Sliding my cupped hands down her flanks, I curled my fingers around her hips, digging into the flesh of her soft, pliant ass. Tightening my grip, I pulled the girl toward me by the hips and then I dove in, nuzzling those wonderful tits, pressing my face into the soft cleavage, nudging the taut mounds with lips and nose, all the while licking, lapping up the sweet tasting wine, drawing my tongue up and over the lush contours while the woman writhed before me, twisting her shoulders in pure, sensual delight.

She arched back offering my greedy lips even more of her feminine pulchritude, while I drew spiraling circles, zeroing in on the fat caps of her pink nipples. I kissed those sensitive tips, taking the protruding stems between my teeth and pulling on them till Sylla gave out with a low, growl of animal pleasure. Then I suckled on that prominent nipple, drawing on it slowly and steadily, with the girl arching back, and writhing in my arms all the while.

My recollection of events after that are a little confused. Somehow we all three ended up on the rug. I remember the image of Sylla, her comely body laid out before me as I straddled her hips on my knees. I leaned forward bringing my upstanding prick up, to rub along its length her wet tits. I had her squeeze them together, imprisoning my rod between the squashed, fleshy mounds, while I moved my hips and spent a little time fucking her tits. Then, just as I was about to shoot off, I moved higher, easing my stiff prick up over her chin and lips, to rub it all over her face. Meanwhile, agile Tomi had slid behind me and, as I crouched down over the other girl, she began paying tribute to my upraised posterior, bringing her lips to my ass, and lavishly licking while I clenched my butt against the maddening tickle. The sudden surge of electric pleasure when the probing tongue touched my anus sent me shooting off all over the pretty face of the supine woman, who closed her eyes but didn't turn away. It was an unforgettable night.

Kimar later asked me if I had enjoyed my fetching companions, and when I responded most enthusiastically, thanking him profusely for his generosity, he asked me if I had ever before had the rare privilege of enjoying both a mother and her daughter at the same time! Perhaps, he added with a sly wink, I'd care to see them make love to each other? Someday he would arrange for the two slaves to perform with each other for my private amusement. It was, he assured me, truly a stimulating sight!

Chapter Seven

THE LORDS OF DISCIPLINE

It was one warm lazy afternoon, as we lounged about in his tent, that Kimar began to tell me about his unique line of work. He was a lonely man, with no one to talk to for long months on end, except for the slaves, and the rather dull louts he employed as overseers. So when he was in his cups with me at his side, an "intelligent man-of-the-world," as he called me, he seemed to want to talk. Kimar was justly proud of his reputation as purveyor of the finest sex slaves to the greatest city in the world, and he wanted me to understand that maintaining that reputation was a constant struggle. It was a sometimes intolerable burden to keep up the increasing demands for both quantity and quality that were insisted upon by the demanding clientele of that insatiable city.

It was bad enough that there were raiders that might pounce on the caravans at any time, that there was the need for constant vigilance, all of which added to the increasing costs of expensive protection. And of course, there were the rigors of the long marches. Through all these problems, he was expected to maintain a quality product, he commiserated with himself, shaking his head at the sad injustice of it all. It was even harder now that the war had cut off slaves from the East. Those were slaves who, having learned submission at the hands of some minor oriental potentate, needed very little training. They would just as readily bend their knee to a Roman master. But with this source of pliable slaves temporarily cut off, and with the demands of Rome increasing, it was to the North and West that he was inevitably forced to turn for new slaves, and these were a very different lot! Wild and unruly, these western barbarians had never learned true obedience. It was up to him to teach them. Now he lowered his voice and confided that there was but one true key to success—discipline. "House slaves and field slaves must learn to obey of course," he explained. They were expected to follow orders and promptly carry out their duties. But sex slaves—they were another matter. They must learn instant and total submission!

The reason that Kimar's slaves were so eagerly sought in Rome, and commanded such exorbitant prices, was found in the long hours spent in training. Kimar was a great believer in very strict discipline, and he had very definite ideas on training slaves. Their relentless training began from the first day when the fresh captives were turned over to him by the army. The new slaves learned that he would tolerate nothing short of perfect obedience. The slave who quickly learned to obey found that her master could be generous, but the slave who refused to submit, and accept her new status graciously, was to find that Kimar was a harsh master of discipline, a maestro, well-versed in the many and ingenious ways of enforcing his iron will.

And as to the matter of punishment, on that subject the old slaver had quite definite, if rather unconventional, views. Of course all slavers made extensive use of the whip to bring their charges into line, but Kimar did so only with the greatest reluctance. A light whip was used sparingly, if at all, especially in the training of the attractive young women who had been earmarked for eventual service to the lords of Rome. Kimar much preferred the use of a stout paddle to enforce discipline, and though it was generally his underlings that took care of such matters, he sometimes chose to take a personal hand in meting out the proper punishment.

"Some men whip their slaves, but I much prefer the paddle. Spanking a slave gives me a great deal of pleasure, while effectively enforcing my will in a way that is painful, but never leaves scars," he explained, quite matter-of-factly.

The firm hand of discipline would only be eased once the girl proved pliant and well-mannered; her obedience, having been put repeatedly to the test, now judged to be satisfactory. Warming to his subject, the old slaver invited me to witness one such punishment about to be carried out on a particularly recalcitrant slave, a Saxon girl whom he had just recently acquired. It seems she was a rather rebellious young lass; her obedience grudging given, her attitude downright surly.

He now invited me to accompany him to the exercise yard where the slaves were being trained. As we approached the fenced-in grassy area that was used for this purpose, a gaggle of naked slave girls pounded past us. Forced to run in the prancing step favored by their handlers, hands clasped behind the neck, knees pumping up high, breasts jogging most delightfully as they passed by. I followed their progress past us and around the track, fascinated by the intriguing view from behind. I was still watching the rear view, entranced, when my attention was abruptly torn away by the shrill cry of a female in distress.

Across the yard from us a tussle had broken out as two of Kimar's men struggled to subdue a squirming female. This was the Saxon girl, a stocky young woman, with a riot of pale tresses and that fell around her face and shoulders. She was a well-built girl, with muscular thighs, and firm high-set breasts, each hefty tit a full handful. Her heels were planted defiantly, and her shoulders twisted trying to shake off the grasp of her guards, while her conical titties jiggled in furious agitation. She kept up her noisy opposition until she was gagged, and then she continued to struggle in a silent but futile attempt to avoid her fate. The burly men had little trouble in manhandling the naked woman. Each one taking an arm, they half dragged, half propelled the braying slave girl to the trestle frame.

Sometimes called the "horse" this sturdy frame was constructed of a padded crossbar supported on thick wooden legs. The crossbar was set at waist height so that a recalcitrant slave could be easily bent over the thickly padded wood. And it was over the crossbar that the business-like overseers now unceremoniously deposited their charge, upending her so that I now saw why Kimar thought I might wish to witness this paddling, for this girl sported a meaty bottom that was perfectly made for just that purpose. Hers was a firm ass: sturdy, solid, and nicely rounded. It was an ass that could absorb much punishment.

One of the slave drivers held her in place over the bar with a large flattened hand placed firmly on the small of her back, while she wiggled her rump and strained upward. The other man dropped to one knee, and clamping a wrist, pulled down on a dangling arm. The girl flailed her legs in screeching protest, kicking up her heels, but the men that held her stepped back quickly. And the heavy hand that pressed against her kept her pinned firmly in place. Now her legs were held, and bound together with strips of leather, tied around the thighs, and again around the calves.

The crouching man was working with swift efficiency now, running twine from the leather wristbands, to a convenient wooden stake sunk in the ground to serve as an anchoring point. Taking up the slack in the line had the effect of drawing the girl still further over the crossbar till her tightly-bound legs hung straight down on the near side, toes pointed down and stiffened so they barely touched the grass.

Now that she was stretched over the bar and held in place, the two overseers stood up and turned to bow briefly to their master. One of them unhooked a paddle that hung from his belt and handed it over to Kimar. This was the short-handled variety with a wide, flat blade of stiffened leather that was thin and pliable. The two capable assistants were now dismissed, as the master would no longer need their services. The Saxon slave was now his, to do with as he would!

Kimar approached the upended miscreant from behind, beckoning me to his side. Quite deliberately, he placed a hand on the served-up buttocks, curving his fingers to fit the rounded domes. The feel of his hand sent his victim mewing into her gag , twitching her hips in anxious protest, the only movement left to her in the helpless situation in which she found herself. The continuing protest brought a smile to the weary face of the old slaver, who took his time feeling her up, running his hand over the twin contours, testing the firm resiliency of those full-fleshed rearcheeks. Obviously pleased in contemplating the task he was about to undertake, the old slaver stepped back and stood eyeing the squirming feminine behind, while lightly tapping his palm with the paddle that he held in his right hand.

Now he took up his position behind, and just to the left, of the dangling legs, tapping the blade of the paddle lightly, squarely across the nicely-presented bottom as he took the measure of his target. He smiled to see the buttocks cringe under the first light kiss of leather. Now he widened his stance, setting his heels in place. Slowly, he drew back the evil paddle and with a sudden snap of the wrist sent it whipping towards the girl's jutting bottom.

THWACK! The snapping blade splattered those jellied mounds, drawing a muffled yelp from the girl, who jerked upward on her bonds as the thudding impact shuddered through her stretched-out form.

Now, Kimar settled into a steady rhythm, spanking the bent-over slave girl, not hard, but with short choppy strokes, rapidly administered, until he had those wobbly rearmounds dancing wildly under the repeated slap of the flexible leather blade. The relentless spanking soon had the girl twitching in fiery agitation, muffled yelps coming from her inverted head with each decisive slap of the juddering mounds.

Eventually, Kimar slowed the pace, pausing somewhat longer between each decisive smack.

THWACK! . . . the pliant rearcheeks flattened and rebounded, leaving a red welt to spread across the twin curving surfaces . . . THWACK! . . . the blade solidly whacked the wobbling mounds . . . THWACK! . . . another firm, decisive stroke, delivered quite dispassionately, by the master slaver, whose eyes were hard and lips were set in a tight, determined line.

The fearful rearcheeks cringed in anticipation of each smack, clenching so that the sides hollowed out as the young Saxon woman steeled herself to meet the next attack. The butt muscles contracted tightly, coiling down to harden the rearmounds, constricting the rearcrack to a deep, narrow slit.

THWACK! Kimar walloped the hardened butt, smacking it squarely across the twin contours with a crisp snap of the wrist. There was an unmistakable howl of outrage, an urgent braying muffed by the wadded rags they had stuffed into her mouth, the gag that was held in place by the silken scarf that bound her head.

Now the slave master paused, and stepped up, to squat down near that inverted head that dangled between the taut, outstretched arms. He reached out to her, cupping her chin and holding it in his fingers as he lifted her head so that he might look into the wide, moist eyes that met his over the silken scarf. I don't know what he saw there. Perhaps it was the hurt, or abject contrition, or maybe a silent plea for mercy, or maybe it was a look of satisfying submission, but whatever it was he saw there, it brought a smile to his lips. He reached under her to cop a quick feel of a dangling breast before rising up and stepping back to once more take up his position. Without further ado, he swung the paddle back in a wide full arc and brought it forward with vigor, ending the swing with a crisp, authoritative snap of the wrist.

THWACK!!! The solid blow landed with authority,

ringing out across the exercise yard, and the muffled shriek it brought was long and wavering. At that he was apparently satisfied. Obviously pleased with his handiwork, the master slaver nodded in grim satisfaction and ran a hand over the warm, flinching rearend. Turning to me, he politely asked if I would like to try my hand. While watching the Saxon girl get spanked had quite an unsettling effect on me, and my swollen penis hung heavy beneath my loincloth, stirring at the sight of those well-punished buttocks, I politely declined. Perhaps I felt some twinge of pity for the chastised slave, who by now, surely had learned her lesson. Kimar shrugged his shoulders and suggested that perhaps some day I would like to take a more active role. I need only say so, and it would be arranged, he assured me!

To complete her punishment, the girl would be left on display in the hot sun for one hour, held in place stretched over the bar so she might contemplate the lesson she had been taught. Salt would be rubbed on her tenderized bottom. Her fiery buttocks, smarting from the angry sting of the wicked paddle, would serve as an object lesson to her cohorts who would be marched slowly past so they might view her throbbing ass and reflect on the price of disobedience.

—⊗⊗⊗—

As Kimar had promised, I was to witness many such exhibitions over the next few months, and to play the disciplinarian's part in more than a few of them. But of these various entertaining spectacles, none was so unforgettable as the time Kimar arranged to have a group of four of his slaves punished simultaneously. It seems that his overseers had uncovered a plot wherein the four young women hoped to sneak away, taking refuge in the woods. There were some transgressions that the slave master would tolerate, viewing them as only minor indiscretions; but attempting to escape was another matter! It was one of those offenses that was taken quite seriously, and any girl caught trying to do so, was inevitably dealt with most severely so that she might be made an example of to those who might be so foolish as to entertain similar notions. As a measure of my growing status as a very special guest, Kimar arranged for a private disciplinary session for the quartet of would-be escapees to be held in his tent.

That evening when I entered his tent I saw that the furniture had been re-arranged. The small couches and pillows had been pushed back along the canvas walls, leaving plenty of room at the center of the huge tent for a sturdy cushioned bench that was low, long, and narrow. A padded board, the same size and shape as the bench, was hinged to it at one end so that the board could be lifted and swung up out of the way.

The purpose of this ingenious arrangement was being demonstrated for me as, sandwiched between the padded surfaces were the four naked malefactors who knelt on hands and knees, their lithe young bodies draped over the bench, bellies pressed down on the leather-covered padding. The top board had been lowered to cross along the shallow curves of the lower backs, and then locked down at the far end, thus clamping the row of kneeling maidens in place. Imprisoned between the two padded surfaces, each girl found herself on hands and knees, unable to move, with shoulders and hips snuggled cozily to her mate's, presenting her own, along with her sisters' naked buttocks for our edification and approval. I noted that each girl had not only been gagged with a wide leather strap tied behind her head, but she was also blindfolded. This latter refinement of the wily slave master's served to increase their helplessness and, by depriving them of knowledge of the approach of their chastisers, introduce the element of surprise into their punishment. A girl might shudder at the thud of the paddle, cringe to hear her sister's muffled cries, sympathize as she squirmed in distress while rubbing anxious shoulders. It would increase her own fearful expectation to know that her time was about to come, but never knowing exactly when the paddle might strike her own vulnerable behind.

I eyed the charming row of girlish bottoms with genuine delight, resonating with a rutting surge of lust that had my manhood responding instantly, quickening, inflamed with the urgency of desire. Momentarily speechless, I beamed my approval, flashing my host my most appreciative grin. He acknowledged my silent compliment with a tilt of his head and put a single finger to his lips to assure my silence. Then, with overblown courtesy he bowed and offered me a paddle, holding it by the blade and presenting the handle to me with a flourish. For this evening's session two wooden paddles had been selected by that consummate connoisseur: sturdy ones with short handles and wide oval blades. Leather paddles imparted more of a sting, but the wooden paddles, with their greater heft, and their stiffer, less pliant blades, delivered a more solid bone-jarring impact.

Still without a word, we moved stealthily, creeping up to take up positions at either end of the row of kneeling women. I stood behind the fourth girl, a slim-hipped slave, whose pertly rounded bottom pointed back at me with saucy impudence. My host went down on one knee to conduct a detailed examination of the first girl in line, enjoying himself by lewdly fondling her helpless ass. I followed his example, squatting down to inspect more closely the girl who was positioned at my end. I adored the symmetry of that small, neat bottom, the way the under curves were well defined so that the mounds jutted out from those slim, tapering thighs. I found that she kept her legs held together squeezing a lightly furred pussy so that it bulged out between the smooth columns of her lithe, young thighs. The sight sent my penis soaring to impossible heights as it came to me that, aside from being ideal for chastisement, the pressing bench would allow a master to take a slave in any number of interesting ways. As I crouched down behind her, contemplating the girl's helpless bottom, I couldn't resist placing a hand on the conveniently-placed rump, curving my fingers to fit one of the pleasingly-contoured cheeks, squeezing lightly.

The sudden and unexpected touch of a masculine hand on her bare ass caused the blindfolded girl to twitch nervously; a tiny whimper of surprise came from her stoppered mouth. Her agitation fired my lust and I slipped my fingers down to touch the softly-furred vulva that peeped out at me from between the clenching thighs. The girl shifted uneasily as my fingers sampled the tiny coils of pubic hair, and pressed tentatively at the closed fleshy gates.

Intrigued, I drew my stiffened index finger along the fur-edged seam and straight up into the deep division between her spasming cheeks giving the helpless girl a sharp thrill that abruptly energized her, causing her to shake her tail in a most enticing way. I looked over to see my host watching me, smiling, giving me an encouraging nod. We were in no hurry to begin the punishment; he saw I was clearly enjoying myself, and nodded. Smiling back at him, I turned to the female slave so nicely at hand.

Eagerly, I clutched that tight-cheeked young bottom in both hands, curling my fingers along the sides, slipping my thumbs into the girls' rear crack so I could pry apart the firm domes to reveal to my eyes her most intimate secret, the pinkish rosette of her newly-exposed anus, embedded in that tallow valley. I contemplated the soft pink of her delicate asshole, and the thought of taking her there fired my lust! The tiny ring of muscle seemed to spasm, winking seductively at me as I watched. With one fingertip I touched her there, pressing lightly, encountering stiff resistance, and getting a muffled grunt from the other end of the slave girl. I smiled to myself. There would be plenty of time later to force the tiny gate, after a proper paddling had made the girl more tractable. I eased out my fingers, and let the straining rearcheeks snap shut; leaving the kneeling slave with a friendly swat on her protruding behind.

Now, still on my knees, I shuffled over to place myself behind the next ass in line, for this one would also be mine before the night was through. Unlike the first girl whose bottom was small and perfectly rounded, the next girl's posterior was more shapely, sculpted with fuller flowing curves that formed a heart-shape. The plump ass seemed to jut back in brazen defiance. I traced the rich swells, drawing my fingertips over the magnificent sweep of those pleasingly feminine buttocks. I thrilled to run my fingers along the curves, savoring the smooth velvety feel of the tautly curved skin, sensing the underlying muscular tension of that well-made bottom. To test its resiliency, I dug my fingers into the softness, pressing till I encountered the underlying firmness of those heavenly mounds. The girl's hips twitched under my loving ministrations, as I freely fondled her supple, fleshy cheeks.

Continuing my examination, I crouched lower and let my cupped hand feel its way along the sculpted contour of an elegantly shaped thigh, staring just behind the knee and letting my fingers shape the swelling lines till they came to the top of the smooth thigh, and there I slid my hand around to sample the flesh of the inner thigh, silken smooth, and warm with sexual heat. The girl shifted uneasily to feel my questing, masculine hand move up between her legs. I slid my hand up to fit my curving fingers to the plump bulge of her soft, furry vulva, a love-purse that was pleasantly warm and inviting; I let my fingers play over its prominent swell. The girl's hips writhed with a sensual excitement that she couldn't possibly control as I lavishly fondled her most intimate parts, the soft folds of her sex. I heard a low moan escape her banded lips, and felt a definite trace of moisture. I rubbed my fingers together, sampling her love juices. The girl was clearly becoming aroused.

I slipped a finger between the slightly protruding lips and found her to be surprisingly wet. A quiver of excitement passed though her body, and she whimpered as the slick lips clung to the finger that was actively exploring her cunt. Her copious flow, and excited reactions, signaled that the healthy young girl might well be on the edge of coming. But my aim was to explore, to stimulate, but not to excite her to orgasm, and so like any good explorer who has made his initial reconnaissance, I moved on, seeking new territory.

I slid my hands up to clasp those fleshy cheeks, and pry them rudely apart, opening her like a fecund peach to expose a cringing anus that tightened reflexively upon being revealed to the world. Holding the girl open with one splayed hand, I applied the fingertip of the other to the flinching rear portal and pressed, persisting in spite of the resistance I felt there, probing with my fingertip, indenting the tight ring of unyielding flesh. An urgent whimper came from the girl as no more than the tip of my finger was gently but persistently inserted up her ass. I diddled her there for a few seconds, while she strained and wiggled, and then I withdrew the offending digit and let the elastic cheeks snap shut, well satisfied with my inspection of her intimate parts. I smiled to myself, pleased at the thought that I might visit that hidden place once again, perhaps after her spanking, for the girl was entirely at my disposal. Having thoroughly examined the miscreants, it was now time to get on with the main event.

I noticed that my cohort had gotten to his feet to take up his position. He stood eyeing his cringing targets, lightly slapping the wooden blade against his palm, his face set in grim determination. I rose to my feet and took up a similar position behind and a little to the side of the second girl's jutting posterior. From this position I could easily reach both tempting targets. Setting my booted heels apart in a widened stance, I sized up the distance to each target, bringing my arm back in a shallow arc to test the range, tightening my grip on the paddle.

Now I took aim at the impudent rearcheeks on the far end, and swung.

THWAP! The wooden blade struck the jutting mounds not hard, but decisively, for I never took Kimar's "punishments" too seriously. I had no wish to hurt the girl, but only to leave her with a sharp reminder, one that would have her sitting down most gingerly for the next week or so. The slave girl screeched her outrage into the gag at the sudden shock of the solid impact. Immediately, I heard an answering, dull thud come from behind me, and I knew that Kimar had found the range on a girl whose big, curvaceous buttocks had clearly attracted him: a most substantial ass that I knew would give him the greatest of pleasure, as each solid impact was followed by a keening yelp.

The resounding smacks rang out repeatedly, punctuated by two muffled cries, as the two paddles came swinging down to flatten the sets of twin mounds, the first smack rapidly followed by another, as we alternated between our dual targets. I watched the way the resilient mounds of the richer, bigger ass bounced back, rebounding nicely at each swiftly delivered slap. And I saw the blade bite deeply into the hard little ass that waited anxiously, cringing at the far end of the line.

THWAP . . . THWAP! . . . THWAP! . . . THWAP! The whipping paddle repeatedly assaulted the solid, impudent ass, sending the small mounds wobbling.

THWAP! . . . THWAP! . . . THWAP! . . . THWAP! The blade smacked the lush soft mounds, sending them wobbling in a wild dance.

Thus we paddled the slave girls, lightly but methodically, using a series of rapid fire shots that had the slaves mewing urgently into their stoppers. Their muted cries, brayed in syncopated rhythm with each crisp smack, blended into a regular cacophony that filled our tented world.

Chapter Eight
THE EAGLE TURNS TO FACE THE NORTH

It was late that summer that ominous reports began to reach our ears of stirrings among the barbarous tribes of the North. Teuton raids on the slave caravans were increasing. Tax officials had been set upon, and now those worthies were refusing to visit the villages without an armed escort. The more civilized tribes were being threatened by the wild men from the north, who were promising that the peaceful tribes would pay a heavy price for cooperating with their Roman overlords. The situation got so bad that it was no longer possible for us to remain sitting idly by. And so I was not surprised when our orders came from Rome. The legion was to take to the field!

I was not looking forward to the hardship of a campaign after the long leisurely days spent so pleasantly at Bernesium. It now seemed inconceivable to me that at some remote time, far away in the safety and comfort of Rome, a young lieutenant had actually complained of boredom and yearned for martial glory. Now facing the immanent prospect of confronting the dreaded Northmen, I felt far less enthusiastic. Still, a Roman soldier must do his duty, and so I ordered preparations be made for our first sally from the comforting security of our cozy well-fortified home.

We hoisted the eagle, and with banners flying we set off heading north; first to the furthest rim of outposts, and then beyond, to enter into the deep, forbidding forests. It was dark and gloomy under the huge trees; the men trudged on in eerie silence. My horse seemed unusually nervous, twitching and snorting, as if he sensed the danger that was all around us. It was less than a day's march into the forest, when our column was first set upon.

The raid was sudden: a fierce, brief attack that came upon us in a flash as we were making our way patiently along the floor of a shallow valley. A piercing blood-curdling scream rang out, and we looked up to see a band of raging pale giants racing down the hillside through the trees, blond hair flying wildly as they flourished the axes, and the heavy clubs these savages preferred as weapons of war. We barely had time to draw our swords and fall automatically into the defensive turtle, shields interlocked. Standing firm, we prepared to stoutly meet the pell mell charge of the fierce barbarians.

In an instant their charge broke over the wall of shields, and they were upon us. The fight was fast and furious, a wild melee of war clubs thudding down on bending shields; Roman broadswords slashing out at the flashing limbs of tussling barbarians. After no more than a few minutes of vicious fighting, the Teuton leader gave out with a shout, and the band fell back, melting away to disappear back into their forest haunts.

It had not been a very determined assault, more of a skirmish really—one that didn't appear to be well planned, but broke upon us helter-skelter. Perhaps a small raiding party had happened to chance upon our column and decided to quickly bloody a Roman nose or two before scampering off; or maybe they'd been sent to find us, to feel us out and test our strength, to see what Rome had sent against them. We bound our wounds and rested. And then we moved on.

The next day our scouts reported smoke coming from a valley up ahead. As we crested the hill we looked down on the smoldering ruins of a devastated village. The few dazed survivors who crawled from the woods when they saw the Roman standard, told the tale of the vengeance of a mighty warlord named Unix, a Teuton chieftain who had demanded tribute, and wrecked havoc on the village when they were unable to pay, slaying the men, burning their huts and taking their women.

In broken Latin, one of the survivors assured us he knew where this Unix had his camp, and he readily offered to lead us there. I talked it over with Sergeant Metelus, and we agreed that the man seemed trustworthy enough. Moreover, it was obvious that we would have to come to terms with Unix eventually, if we were to subdue his revolt, and so we decided to lay plans for an attack. We would move quickly, but with caution, throwing out scouts before us and stealthily making our way towards the barbarian encampment, hoping the element of surprise might, this time, be on *our* side.

We marched all that day, and well into the night. And it was some time after noon on the second day when our guide cautioned us to move more quietly, as we were getting closer to the enemy camp. I had the men wait while the

Sergeant and I accompanied our guide, scrambling through a narrow defile and onto a rocky ledge that looked down on the sprawling enemy camp. We crept up behind some rocks, and cautiously raised our heads.

The scene below was peaceful. There were campfires burning; blond women clustered about them, while children played at a stream nearby. At one end of the camp, there were carts piled high with loot, and a band of defeated captives sat dejectedly, heads hung low, idly guarded by a single warrior. Probably taken in some recent raid, these hapless men and women were now the slaves of this upstart and his men. We noticed that they had the same crude dress and blond appearance as their captors. Unix was obviously making war on other Germanic tribes as he struggled to establish his supremacy over the northern people. We counted several scores of warriors, most of them unarmed, although their arms were stacked near by. These fighting men were not deployed for defense. Here and there, an occasional guard had been posted, but the camp was clearly not on alert.

It seemed inconceivable to me; the gods must be with us! Surely by now the raiding party must have warned them of the presence of a Roman column in their own backyard, but there was a curious air of lax tranquility about the barbarian encampment. It was as though they were oblivious to any danger; or perhaps they were so confident of their strength that they had become arrogant, rashly disregarding any warnings they may have had.

Carefully, we made our way back to where my men waited hidden behind the rocks, and there we planned our attack. Because the camp lay in the middle of a large plain, we would be seen as soon as we emerged from the rocks, thus giving our enemy plenty of time to spread the alarm and rush to arms to meet our charge. Therefore, we would split our force.

I would lead a contingent down the defile, tumbling across the plain, brandishing our swords, shouting and charging with a great clamor. As soon as the Teuton warriors rushed onto the field to meet us, we would turn, as though in sudden panic, and flee back towards the rocks. Once we had the over-confident enemy strung out and racing eagerly across the plain, we would suddenly stop and turn on them, while Sergeant Meletus, leading the main body of our men, would at that moment fall on them from their flank. The maneuver took disciplined timing, but my troops had practiced it many times; they knew what they had to do.

The charge went as planned; the alarmed barbarians scurried for their weapons and rushed out onto the plain. We feigned cowardice at the fierceness of their charge, and let them chase us. Then at my signal, we dug in our heels and wheeled about, preparing to meet our onrushing enemy. We clashed and immediately found ourselves in a furious fight, swords flashing and clubs swinging wildly as we fought toe to toe. I managed an anxious look to the surrounding rim of rocks just in time to see Meletus with the main body cresting a small hill to begin their charge.

At that point my attention was fully occupied by a blond giant, who grabbed me by the ankle and pulled me from my mount. I hit the ground with a thud, momentarily stunned, and he screamed and swung a murderous mace at my head, which I managed to duck away from at the last second. It hit the ground next to my ear with a bone-jarring thud. I spun over, and leapt to my feet, just as the second blow came swinging my way. This time he swung in a high circle, leaving himself open. I saw my chance and I took it, lunging with my blade to catch him under the arm and stab upward straight into his chest. With a sharp cry the big man went down, nearly tearing the sword out of my hand as his massive body twisted and fell. My head was singing as I pulled the sword free in a geyser of blood and swung around, bloody sword at the ready.

I was much too busy to keep track of the battle, but I saw that our comrades had joined us, and now we had the enemy closed in a loose pincer. From somewhere a horn sounded, and I realized there was a second force of the enemy who appeared suddenly, hidden reserves perhaps who were now rushing to join the fray. Maybe we had been tricked, but I had no time to think about that, as I found myself slashing furiously, severing limbs and felling blond warriors left and right as I hacked my way through the press of desperate fighting men.

For a while we struggled in a battle where neither side would yield. Then slowly, we began to surge forward, and the barbarian line faltered and then began to break up. Suddenly, it cracked, dissolving into small islands of savages, still fighting desperately even as their comrades began to desert them, at first a few, then in droves, falling back, turning and running from the terrible battle. My men sensed that victory was ours and at their triumphant cry, chased after the stricken foe, scattering them as they ran for the safety of the woods.

I saw the blond chieftain holding his own under his standard of animal pelts, and made my way toward him, as his guards fell around him one after the other. The noose of legionnaires was getting tighter around the Teuton standard, when somehow the mighty warrior managed to tear himself away from our grasp and taking a few of his men with him, fled towards the defile and possible escape. I motioned for a party of legionnaires to come with me and we went off in hot pursuit. It took us a while, chasing the little band through the hills, till at last we managed to corner our foe with his back against the face of a cliff.

I stood facing the powerful well-built warrior, and I had no doubt—this was Unix, their chieftain. He stood taller than the other men, his loincloth torn and bloody, the hard muscles of his torso sheened with sweat and dripping with blood that trickled down from a sword wound that had been opened at his side. But he was not defeated. His eyes were fierce and blue, and he trembled with excitement as he wheeled around to face us. His hands and arms were bloody from the slaughter and he had lost his shield, but his right hand still held the wicked battleaxe, its deadly blade gleaming bright red. I shouted for him to yield, even though I knew that a proud barbarian like this would never allow himself to be taken alive to be hauled back to Rome in a cage.

He looked at me for a moment above the fray, and then, with a fierce shout, plunged towards me, swinging his ax wildly. It was no contest, for by now the Teuton chieftain had lost his few remaining companions, and the big man went down alone under the weight of our numbers, swinging defiantly at his pursuers till the very end.

By the time we made our way back to the scene of the battle, the last remnants of the enemy were being dispatched. We heard the pitiful cries of the wounded as the swords came down; the smell of blood was strong in the air. Parties of soldiers had begun looting the enemy camp, gathering the captured booty that was now ours, rounding up the women and children, sorting out those that would be taken to serve Rome. I found my trusty Sergeant, in the middle of organizing the mopping up operations.

He stood talking to a Teuton girl: a slender reed of a girl, fair featured and small-breasted, her name was Minta. The young woman had been a slave of Unix, and now she would be a slave of Rome, perhaps a most valuable slave as the clever girl spoke Latin, as well as Gaullic and the Germanic tongue of the Teutons. For the first time since the onset of the battle I looked at my Sergeant and smiled, and he smiled back, and we stood there saying not a word, smiling at one another, bloody and dirty and weary but triumphant at this, our first victory, and a most decisive one at that!

As we were congratulating ourselves, a shrill scream caused me to spin around just in time to see a crazed woman flying at me from behind one of the wagons. She was brandishing a nasty dagger over her head and would surely have struck me, had not Metelus alertly stuck out his foot to trip her, sending her sprawling across the grass. Her weapon was knocked from her grasp by the impact, but she quickly got to her hands and knees to scramble after the knife when two of my men pounced on her. She howled her outrage and struggled under them, screaming all the while in that guttural tongue of the northmen. I knew only a few words, but I recognized the Teuton words for "Roman pigs."

She was expertly subdued, and one of the men who knelt on her with his knee pressed between her shoulders, gathered up a fistful of long blond hair and lifted back her head, exposing her throat while he drew his dagger. He would have dispatched her on the spot, had I not stopped him with drawn dagger in mid-air. At my command the soldiers got the would-be assassin to her feet and brought her to me. Holding her firmly by the arms they dragged her before me.

She was a magnificent blond animal! Even though her face was contorted with sizzling rage, I could see she possessed those proud Nordic features of her kind. Hers was a face of rare beauty, the angular plains of her cheeks defined by fine high-set cheekbones, a long sculpted nose with flaring nostrils, precise lips and those big eyes of icy blue that, flashing in insolence and cold anger, penetrated to the soul. Her hair was wild and matted, but it had the quality of pure spun gold. Hanging in sheets of silvery blond, it fell in bangs across her forehead, and framed her long oval face, as she stood before me, twisting in the painful grip of her grim guards.

As she was brought face to face with her new Roman master, she screamed her defiance, repeating the same words again and again. Minta translated. "Kill me! Kill me!" the young woman demanded. She wished only to die, for she swore she would rather face death than submit to a Roman. Of course, I had no intention of granting that proud beauty her wish, for it would be a tragedy indeed to slay such a creature who had so obviously been made to give pleasure to men.

Now, I regarded her blazing eyes, and let my gaze deliberately drop to take in that tall, handsome blond body. Her single garment was a roughhewn tunic of animal hide that hung from her shoulders to mid-thigh and was belted at the waist with a thin strip of leather. I asked her name and waited while Minta translated. She said nothing, but eyed me coldly. I nodded to the guard who stood behind her and applying pressure to her arm, we got to her spit out her name: Helva.

I nodded, then ordered the men to strip her, pulling off the tunic, ripping off the loincloth she wore underneath so that she was left standing before me in nothing but her sandals. For a moment, I stood regarding her long-limbed body. Her breasts were not large, but the gentle swells were so tautly drawn that they stood out like thickened disks, circles of *bas relief* standing out on her exquisitely made chest with wide pink nipples that were precisely centered. Between long, lean thighs, a softly mounded pubis waited invitingly, sporting a thick fleece of silvery gold, that only half hid the thick pink labia that nestled in its profusion of tiny curls.

I had the guards force the big blonde to her knees. Then I strode closer, to stand over the naked woman as she knelt there before me, head hung low. I drop a hand to her head, and was pleased to feel the silkiness of that fine blond hair. I couldn't resist taking a strand to rub between my fingers. Then, abruptly digging into the silken mass, I clenched a fistful and pulled back her head, forcing my blond captive to look up at me. I looked down into those resentful blue eyes and I told her of her fate. Her feelings in the matter were of not the slightest concern to me, I explained, while Minta translated my words.

She would live, but her life would no longer be hers. From this day forward, she was a slave of Rome. As such she must learn to serve the pleasure of her masters. To do, without question, whatever was demanded of her. Above all, she must learn obedience. And if she learned well, and became a good little slave, she would be treated well, but if she was a bad girl, then she would surely be punished. At that, I twisted the handful of hair, bringing pain to her eyes, and the girl spat at me! I laughed and tightened my grip, hurting her, till she cried out. Then I tossed her head down, and had the men stake her out. This fiery hellcat must be tamed, her pride broken, her will bent, her body taken and enjoyed by the Romans she so thoroughly feared and despised.

The men made quick work of it, even though she continued to struggle in vain. There were four of them, one at each limb, and they easily held her down while the stakes were driven into the ground and her arms and legs outstretched to be tied in place. Her constant screeching annoyed me, and I had her gagged. That helped, although her muffled keening continued unabated for a while, till it eventually trailed off in helpless frustration.

Now she lay quiet. The sight of the naked blonde, spread-eagled on the ground, every sinew of her long, streamlined body pulled taut by the restraints that bound her wrists and ankles, brought fire to my loins. A surge of lust shot through me, and my cock twitched with eager expectation. The sinews of her arms and legs took much of the strain, drawing taut her sleek torso and stretching her tits into two elongated, slightly flattened, swells crowned with choice nipples that were pertly erect; the bottom ridge of her ribcage was dimly visible under the tightly stretched skin, and below that, a slight hollow had been formed as the skin of her belly was pulled taut as a drum between the points of her prominent hipbones. My eyes were drawn to the splay of pale, silvery pussyfur that marked the mounded pubis, the little fleshy pad that sat there so soft and inviting, the stretched-open vagina, dark fleshy lips agape, showing the brighter slick folds of pink inside. I wanted to curl my fingers up between her outstretched legs and shove them up her splayed-open cunt while palming her Venus mound, pleasuring her till she was maddened by lust. I wanted to see this proud savage's body betray her as she squirmed with the heat of helpless arousal. The very thought had my prick stirring, swelling, and blossoming forth in full erection as I contemplated that superb specimen. But I would reserve that sweet pleasure for some later time. For now, she would entertain the troops.

This method was used to initiate those women captives destined to spend their days in army brothels. On several occasions, I had seen an entire cohort of legionnaires being serviced in just this manner. But this slave must be used more carefully. I meant to use our prized captive as a reward for my heroes. Metelus was given the task of selecting those lucky men who had especially proven themselves in battle. Naturally, I allowed him to have her first, rewarding him for his steadfast loyalty and courage. Of course, he politely deferred to me, but I told him I was content to wait. I assured him, I meant to have her too, but not just yet . . . and not in the same manner as my men.

Now, the lusty legionnaires began to line up, grinning and laughing in ribald good humor, hugely pleased with their unexpected good fortune. And when our captive fully realized what was about to happen, her blue eyes grew wide with alarm over the gag, and the muffled braying started all over again. She yanked on her bounds and squirmed, but there was very little she could do and her agitated movements only served to further inflame the randy men who huddled around her, sporting mighty erections.

The good Sergeant dropped on his knees between those magnificent wide-spread legs. He lifted his clothes in front, and drew out his well-endowed equipment, letting her see his splendid manhood in its fully aroused state as he knelt upright before her. He reached up to run his hands over that splendid body, roughly mauling her served-up tits and then, too excited to wait any more, he guided his prick into her gaping pussy, and fell on her. Helva's pneumatic body seemed to bounce under his full weight; the big, thick prick slid up her cunt, drawing a deep, throaty groan.

We watched him fuck her, while she threw back her blond head and shut her eyes, receiving the savage pounding as the randy noncom worked himself up to a lust-driven frenzy, pumping into her, bucking furiously. It took only a few seconds of this intense fucking till he tossed back his head, his body stiffening back into an arc, and straining upward, came with a long strangled cry. We watched him wearily dismount, depleted, and breathing heavily. His softening prick, still throbbing, carelessly dribbled the last trickles of ropy sperm on the girl's open thighs. He staggered away to collapse in a heap, while the second man eagerly knelt down to take his place. And so it went, one after the other, until the sex-ravaged woman had accommodated my N.C.O. and six of my best men.

Now I stood over her, looking down into those dazed blue eyes, and realized that all the savage anger had been beaten out of her. There was no loud braying now, no frantic twisting in her bounds. Her splayed cunt twitched, the pinkish folds throbbing in the aftermath of her multiple orgasms, oozing a trickle of Roman seed, mixed with her own copious spendings. I placed a sandaled foot between her crotch and nudged her well-used sex with my toes. The blond girl groaned, but otherwise lay inert, thoroughly drained, without the least shred of resistance when my men loosened her bounds, only to flip her limp body over and re-tie her, this time stretched out facedown.

At last, for the first time since she had been taken prisoner, I was able to fully appreciate the beauty of Helva's lush naked bottom—a perfectly splendid ass, nicely-curved twin mounds that swept up in the most pleasing invitation. It was my turn to get my hand on that healthy, young body!

Kneeling between her out-stretched legs, I used both hands to thoroughly savor the sinuous lines of the barbarian's long streamlined body, running them up the backs of those taut-muscled calves, relishing the satiny smoothness of those elegantly curved legs. I followed the sleek contours up to the hollows behind the knees, and beyond, traveling up the smooth skin at the back of her tapering thighs. My fingertips sampled the silken band of flesh high up along her inner thigh and then I traveled a few inches higher and my questing fingers were exploring the soft purse of her thick wet labia. I pressed along the heated cove of Venus, feeling my way along those rubbery, slick lips, dipping a finger into that honey pot, and getting a soft shuddering moan from the skewered blonde. I withdrew my sticky finger and ran it up the perineum, and then drew it along the crack of Helva's handsome ass, while my captive twitched uncontrollably in a simmering excitement. In spite of herself, the girl wiggled, thrilled by the stab of pleasure as my finger probed between the lips of her cunt.

And now I spent a few leisurely moments, delighting in the warm, satiny feel of Helva's magnificent ass. I lovingly fondled those twin, shapely cheeks, so neatly symmetrical, so breathtakingly perfect: the soft silkiness, the plaint resiliency, the deep inner firmness. I couldn't resist cupping my hand, and whacking that provocative ass of hers, delivering a solid slap to test the bouncy resiliency of those meaty mounds. Helva's head jerked up in shocked reflex, and she yanked on her bounds, clenching her fists in spasms of rage. I calmly laid my flattened hand on the small of her back and moving it slowly in a deep, massaging caress, brought it up the sweeping slopes to clutch a single rubbery cheek, and squeeze firmly, digging my fingers into her hidden valley, and clutching a handful of cheek in a tight grip. And in that way, I leisurely played with Helva's superb bottom, feeling her up, mauling, kneading those twin mounds to my heart's content, while the helpless girl squirmed, caught in rising sensual heat, her healthy young body responding instinctively to the touch of a man.

Her excited squirming had gotten me hard as a rock, my prick aching, demanding satisfaction. I moved my clothes up out of the way and brought my erect manhood up along her crack, pressing my loins down against those heavenly pillows, my prick snuggling happily between them, as I rubbed it up and down that hot, tight valley.

Easing off, I clasp her butt, and slipping my thumbs into the crease, I pried her open so I might examine her anus. I touched my finger to her there, to find her rear entrance warm and dry, and incredibly tight. The little rosette stubbornly resisted the pressure of my stiff, probing finger. Suddenly angry, I slapped her rump, hard.

"You have a lot to learn my beauty," I muttered, leaning down to bring my lips close to her ear.

Now, I made some extra preparations for my next attempt to storm that clenching citadel. First, I called for rolled blankets to be placed under her loins. This additional padding had the effect of pulling the outstretched limbs even more tightly and elevating her heightened rearend to even greater prominence. Next, I had them bring us some oil, and this was poured in a generous stream down her rear divide while I held her cringing cheeks apart. I worked some oil into the cringing rear portal, and rubbed a bit on my hardened cock.

At last, I was ready to resume my place up between her legs. Holding her open with one splayed hand, I guided my prick to its target. With increasing excitement I held her open, and pressed down on her anus; the girl cried out to feel my determined assault. Suddenly furious, I stabbed at the clenched ring of muscle, intent on forcing the tiny gate, pressing inexorably, till I felt the portal begin to yield to me. I slapped her butt, again and again, smacking her smartly as I kept up my unrelenting pressure. My captive howled her outrage into her gag; I slipped in and gained a quick inch or so. The tiny ring of muscle that had loosened for an instant now contracted immediately as I gained entrance, but I was in! Now I fell forward, letting her take the fullness of my weight, while driving my rigid cock smoothly right up her curvaceous ass. The barbarian shook her blond mane in frantic refusal; a soft gurgling sound came out from around the gag,

I savored the sweet tightness I found there, the way the savaged asshole clenched me, the way her shifting mounds felt pressed solidly against my hips. I let my hips rock forward, delighting in the bouncy resiliency of Helva's wonderful ass, while a strangled groan escaped from my impaled captive.

Soon I was fucking the blond barbarian's asshole, pumping in slow, even strokes, pulling out almost to the very tip, only to lunge in, in a full, deep plunge, that buried my sword up to the hilt in her churning butt. The little anus clung tightly to my shaft, sucking me in as I drew back. Fired with lust, I speeded up my cadence, pumping into her, more quickly now, my prick pistoning in and out with brisk, short strokes. Soon I was raging out of control, bucking furiously, crazed with lust and fucking my beautiful blond captive's churning ass with wild abandon, while my randy men cheered me on. I felt the teasing trickle of pleasure rising up in my loins; felt its gathering power, till it became a mighty surge of lust, a raging, unstoppable geyser that erupted into the Teuton's undulating ass, sending jets of Roman seed deep into her barbarian bowels. The explosion of pleasure shook me as I fired my essence into that bounding ass. I felt her inner heat, her tightening on me as if her asshole were milking my throbbing cock dry, and I fell back, extracting my still pulsating prick to let the last dribbles of my sperm decorate that pretty rump.

Well satisfied that our new slave had been properly introduced to her subservient status, I felt that one further refinement might be added as I stared thoughtfully at that twitching ass. Calling Minta over I had her crouch down by the head of the pinioned slave, to translate my words. I told her that her Roman master would undoubtedly want to revisit that choice rearend of hers, and there was considerable room for improvement there. Therefore, I would see to it that a proper butt plug was inserted, to exercise that portal, and to remind her that she must be much more accommodating in the future.

And at my command, a squat, wooden plug was quickly fashioned, oiled, and promptly inserted in the ravaged anus of the outstretched blond girl, while she whimpered plaintively from behind her gag. And that was how she spent her first night as a captive of Rome. Spread-eagled and tied down, the rude butt plug lodged well up her behind, the squat end left to jut out from between clenching cheeks, moving each time she contracted her buttocks, the well-fucked woman could do nothing, but contemplate her fate. The other captives were brought over to see her in this sorry state, so they too might reflect on the price of obstinacy to the will of Rome.

Chapter Nine

TAMING THE BLOND BARBARIAN

In Bernesium it is said the people still talk of my triumphant return. A glorious day it was, with banners flying, crowds cheering, slaves marching in bondage and, trailing behind me, the fairest captive of them all, a magnificent blond barbarian, trussed up and swinging from a pole. When we were yet a day out of town, I had my men prepare Helva for my triumphal entry. She was made to lie face down on the ground; her arms were pulled back, and her legs bent at the knees so that wrists might be bound to her ankles, one loop of rawhide binding all four limbs together. This method of tying her up, pulled her body back till it was lightly bowed. Now a long, smooth, wooden pole was passed under her bound wrists and ankles; a soldier at each end hoisted it up, raising our captive so that her long body hung swaying beneath the pole, nipples pointing to the ground. In this ignominious manner, my blond beauty was paraded through the village behind my horse, her place in the column a sign of her special status, telling the world that the commander had claimed her as his own personal sex slave.

Next followed our victorious troops, smiling and waving to the crowd of townspeople; and bringing up the rear the rest of the slaves, marching naked with hands bound before them; a sprinkling of young men and boys, and then a score or more of female slaves, blond, Nordic women whose fair features were much admired by the gaping crowd, murmuring in wonder as they passed by.

The slaves were taken to the penned-in area used by the slavers just west of town, where they would be further sorted out. They would be held there to await the arrival of Kimar, for they would be sold to him (and to no other passing slaver in accordance with our agreement). For this exclusive consideration, I would receive a princely sum, over and above the sale price which would, of course, have to be reported to Rome. It goes without saying that a few captives might be held back, saved from the old slaver's clutches to be reserved for my personal use. I also meant to make a gift of one or two to Gratius for his kind hospitality in the past. I had not mentioned it to him, but I knew he was hopeful of such a largess once he had laid his greedy eyes on the coffle of fair-haired slave girls.

Upon my triumphant return, he had been the first to rush out and greet me, welcoming me back with gushing enthusiasm, and quite generously placing his House at my disposal. In fact, he went so far as to insist that I move out of my modest quarters at the fort, to take up residence in one wing of his palatial estate, for I was truly a hero of Rome and he would be much honored to have me as his guest. I knew he had at least one eye on my prize captives, but I graciously accepted, sure that some sort of deal was in the making.

I selected three of my newly-acquired slave girls to accompany me to my new quarters: Helva, of course; clever Minta, who had proven to be quite useful as a translator, and who, it turned out, showed surprising enthusiasm as a sprightly sex slave; and a third girl, a slender Germanic beauty named Iryna. Of the same delicate-boned and long-limbed race, Iryna was a bit younger and not quite as tall as the statuesque Helva, but there was something about her slim thighs, and lean, youthful body that powerfully stirred me. I noticed her cool beauty as she marched in line, head held high, pale blue eyes on some distant horizon: The small blond face with those neat, precise features, the bright, straw-colored hair that fell in smooth sheets to her shoulders, the slender limbs, and lithe torso with the most appealing little breasts: two small taut globes with slightly up-tilted nipples that stood up, perky and expectant. This was the trio I took with me when I left the cold and drafty fort, and moved in to a comfortable suite of spacious rooms overlooking the lake.

That evening I had my new sex slaves brought to the baths. We all needed to be cleaned up after the long march, and spending a few leisurely hours in the warm scented air of Gratius' baths seemed the ideal way to ease away the aches and pains of the campaign. Stream was rising from the shallow pools, the warm air rich with the aroma of fragrant oils and spiced perfumes as I entered to find my girls waiting for me. As I had ordered, the three waited on their knees, sitting back on their heels, lined up in a row. They had been scrubbed and cleaned and, as befitted their new status, each wore the high leather collar, along with the wrist and ankle bands of a sex slave.

Helva knelt erect on the left. Her hair was still wet, and

the crown of her blond head, which was tilted down, gleamed like burnished gold. She knelt with eyes downcast, for she would not meet my gaze unless I demanded it. I watched her circular breasts rise and fall in gentle undulations; coral pink nipples moist and taut. Beside her, Iryna waited with head held high, her damp blond hair richly dark, hung lank to her neck and softly sloping shoulders. She was watching me alertly, her blue eyes following my every move. Her breasts, like the rest of her slim torso was pale white, especially when contrasted against the even tan of her limbs—two small white globes, each neat handful capped by those impertinent nipples.

At the other end, Minta knelt with head bowed respectfully. In light of her willing and cooperative attitude, and her status as my official translator, she had been given one of the gauzy tunics worn by Gratius' house slaves while her two fellow slaves, unruly, and not yet trained, were of course, kept totally naked. I had come to appreciate this sprightly girl on the homeward march. She was eager to please, and far from sharing the other girls' hatred of Rome, she was warmly affectionate and always willing toward its representative. I learned that although she was a German, she came from a different tribe than the others. She had been captured in one of Unix' raids, and given to the imperious Helva, who had treated her with contempt. Naturally, she was overjoyed to find her proud mistress had now been reduced to the level of a mere sex slave, both women equal in their subservience to their Roman master.

Now I studied that slightly-built, nubile body; those floppy titties, small crescent shaped breasts that invited the touch. I delighted in sampling those charming little tits by rubbing them between my fingers, pulling on the elastic flesh till the girl squealed, savoring their dreamy feel, for the pale, pliant skin was smooth as silk. The shallow breasts were tipped with neat caps and protruding nipples, precisely made nubbins, tiny stems that stuck out boldly. Her rich blond hair was also damp, a deep dark gold, streaked with a flavor of rich caramel, that she wore pulled back and tied so as to resemble a pony's tail, in the Gaullic manner. I looked at her, with the filmy tunic wetly plastered to that straight, sinewy figure and, not for the first time, felt a definite stirring of lust.

I ordered the slaves to rise up off their haunches and hold themselves erect, kneeling, with back perfectly straight, hands behind their necks in a presentation position often used by Kimar to show off a girl's best attributes. Then, while the other two held the mandated pose, I summoned Minta to attend me. The bright girl had quickly learned the proper way to undress her lord and master, and I delighted in the feel of her soft knowing hands as they passed over my body, undoing clasps and drawing off my belt. She removed my tunic and undid my loincloth, careful not to touch my swelling manhood, for such a move without my expressed permission would amount to gross impertinence! Then I eased back onto one of the couches, while my dutiful slave bent over me to untie the straps of my sandals, and slip them off my naked feet.

Once undressed, I stepped down into one of the inviting pools of warm water. I invited Minta to join me, and she swiftly drew off her tunic, stripping her narrow hipless form to bare the clean lines of the smooth front and the slight rises of her crescent shaped titties that perched so proudly on her willowy chest. Her pussy, small and inviting, was a lightly furred mound hazed with a pale soft down; the pink lips small, and puckered in a neat tuck. I summoned Iryna to join us in the bath. The two slave girls would bathe me while I kept Helva on her knees before me so that I might enjoy the pleasure of seeing her nude beauty while I gave myself up to the tender ministrations of my handmaidens.

Wading up to my knees in the water, I turned my back to Iryna while offering my front to Minta, and the girls started to work on me, rubbing all over my nude body, first with invigorating stiff brushes, then with soft wet washcloths. Minta worked with her usual enthusiasm, methodically covering every inch of skin. I watched her scrub her way across my chest, taking her time there, pausing to play with the wet chest hairs, toying with my nipples, her nimble fingers working their way down my flinching belly, teasing along to skirt the edge of my pubic hair. I allowed her to wash my masculine equipment but cautioned her to be quick about it, as I was already stiffening, and I didn't want to be brought to climax so soon in the game.

Iryna, meanwhile, was moving her hands over the knotted muscles of my back and shoulders, pressing lightly. Her hands, moving dutifully but indifferently, lacked the enthusiasm of her sister's who was presently kneeling before me, impishly lifting my scrotum to scour under my balls, her small, wet face upturned, and smiling at me. Even when I leaned down to present my butt for Iryna's attention, her hands simply passed over my proffered cheeks in a perfunctory manner. I decided the girl could benefit from a good dose of salts under her tail, and I would see to it!

I climbed out of the water and had the slaves wrap me in scented towels, and then methodically rub dry my body.

Next, I reclined naked on the couch, laying on my side while the slave girls brought scented oils to rub into my skin. Iryna knelt behind me massaging my back, while Minta's clever fingers once more explored the front of my body. As these small feminine hands worked their wonders on my tired and aching muscles, I gazed at the kneeling blonde before me, arms raised and elbows back, brazenly showing me her breasts while her striking face remained passive and expressionless.

"Beauty," I called her, for such was the name I'd chosen for her, "Play with yourself!"

The blond head turned in my direction at the sound of her slave name, which she recognized by now. The pale blue eyes, which she now turned on me, held a look of loathing; implacable hatred, filled with cold insolence. She had picked up a few words of Latin; I had ordered that she was to learn our tongue quickly. But just to be sure she understood, I now had Minta translate for me.

"Tell her I want to see her play with herself," I instructed cheerfully. "Her tits . . . and her pussy, too! I want to watch while she does it." I knew my proud captive would find the orders distasteful, might even refuse. But I meant to press her, to constantly test her obedience, till she learned to obey even the most perversely outrageous orders, and to do so with alacrity. Minta seemed to thoroughly enjoy repeating my orders in the harsh Germanic tongue.

For a long moment I met the smoldering anger in those steely blue eyes and we held each other's unflinching gaze. It was the blonde who moved first, tilting her head down under my unrelenting glare. I saw her shoulders deflate in a tiny sigh of resignation. Then she brought her hands up to place them over her softly mounded tits.

Pressing lightly she began to move the mounds of flesh with her joined fingers, rubbing them in slow circles, doing what I had ordered, but obviously without much in the way of enthusiasm.

"Better than that! Go on, feel yourself up!" I shouted impatiently.

Obediently, the long, narrow fingers closed on those lovely breasts and she curved her palms to cup herself, fondling the tittie-flesh, moving it more lavishly now, though her movements still had a certain mechanical quality.

I found the sight of the pretty blonde fondling her own tits to be highly erotic, even though she did her best to suppress any sign of excitement on her part. She meant to prove to me that, while she could be made to perform for me, she would take no pleasure in such perverse acts. I wasn't sure that was the case however, for even now her healthy young body was starting to betray her. By close observation one could discern that her sensate nipples were beginning to emerge from their disks of crinkled flesh, stiffening under the mild stimulation they enjoyed.

"Your nipples . . . play with your nipples!" I urged, barely managing to suppress my wild excitement. My voice, heavily laden with passion, had gone suddenly hoarse.

I watched as those slender fingers delicately took each pink tip between them in a pincer movement and the girl pinched her nipples, rolling the little buds between thumbs and forefingers.

"Pull on them," I hissed.

Still holding herself erect, the blank expression on her pale blond face never wavering, the young woman obediently plucked the burgeoning stems, pulling the pliant flesh, twisting the captive nipples that darkened and blossomed under all this attention. I ordered her to wet her fingers in her mouth, and to continue her efforts till she had her emerging nipples fully erected, and only then did I allow her to quit.

"Enough! Now your pussy! Spread your legs, my Beauty, and play with yourself!" I managed to get out, though my voice cracked under the strain. Minta's translation held an unmistakable note of glee.

The agile fingers quit the sensitive nipples; I smiled to see those fully expanded tips standing proud, glistening and hard with arousal. I watched the girl shift to widen her knees, and bring both hands down, as the fingers nosed along the sides of her blond vulva. Her slithering hands become bolder as they edged closer to her sex. It was the right hand that moved in so that she might hold herself, with one hand cupped protectively over her blond pubis.

The hand moved slowly, rubbing sensuously, stirring the first lapping waves of self-pleasure. I studied those Nordic features more closely, alert for the first signs that all this self stimulation was getting to her. There was a definite tinge of pink along the ridges of her cheekbones as she experienced the first flush of arousal, while she rubbed along the converging sides of her pubis. Her eyes were half-lidded now, the pretty lashes lowered, and I saw her work her lips, the tongue peeking out to quickly pass over them as her right hand slid down between her legs to capture her blond sex. I watched her hand closing and opening rhythmically, as the blond barbarian squeezed and palmed her pubic mound. Her breathing deepened, and her shoulders twisted under the delicious waves of pleasure she was generating in her hot treasure box.

I passed a hand across my brow to find it hot and damp, for the steamy solo performance was certainly getting to me. My cock stood upright, throbbing with eagerness, straining taut as a bowstring, aching with desire.

"Sit back on your heels, and open your legs . . . wider, all the way, like the German whore you are!" I ordered harshly. The girl hesitated, but she did as I commanded, shifting back, spreading open her thighs to show me her pink pussy.

"Now, get a finger in there, two fingers . . . I want to see you fuck yourself!"

Her head snapped up, her eyes fluttered open, and she looked up at me. Suddenly, I saw those questioning eyes harden. She hesitated, teetering on the verge of outright refusal. But even if she thought better of it and decided to comply it was too late, for even her slight hesitation was enough to condemn her to a proper dose of punishment. For a moment we waited, and all time stood still. Then she let her head drop and her hands fall uselessly to her side, passively refusing to accede to my perverse wish. This was what I had been waiting for.

"You refuse?" The blond head never moved. "Then I'm afraid you must learn the cost of disobedience. Kneel up now . . . hands behind your head!"

Once more this exquisite, young woman assumed the presentation position, slowly closing her knees, straightening up, bringing her hands up to the back of her neck. I called Minta to me and whispered my instructions in her ear, watching her smile widen into an evil grin as she realized what I had in mind. She was surprisingly enthusiastic in carrying out her task. Gathering up some rawhide strips, she stepped up behind the kneeling blonde and roughly pulled her arms down to tie her hands behind her. This was efficiently done as the slaves' wrist cuffs had, sewn in them, a set of brass rings. A line running through the rings could be quickly knotted as a convenient method for securing a slave's wrists together.

Next, my captive was gagged, her mouth stuffed with a damp washcloth. She was forced to accept the packing by the simple expedient of having Minta pinch a nipple, so that when the Helva gasped in surprise, the wadded cloth was rudely forced between her gaping jaws. A wide leather strap tied around her head imprisoned the folds of blond hair, and held the packing in place in her gaping mouth. Little Minta, always helpful, was beaming, extremely proud of her handiwork as she pulled the kneeling girl to her feet, and led her over to present her to me.

Helva seemed surprisingly docile as, with hands tied behind her back, she let herself be led to me by the smaller girl. Yet even though she seemed willing to accept her fate and allow her body to be used for my pleasures, the cold anger in her eyes still smoldered with the same implacable hatred. For a moment I studied those hard eyes that gazed at me from above the strap, then I curtly nodded, and Minta turned our captive around, and forced her to her knees, so she was left kneeling in front of one of the low couches. With a rude shove the big blonde was toppled forward to lay upended over the couch.

It must have been the memories of her own abject slavery at the hands Unix, when Minta was forced to serve the haughty blonde, that brought such obvious pleasure to her small, astonished face when I handed her a paddle and ordered her to use it on her former mistress' served-up ass. The girl could hardly believe her good fortune!

Now, while she took her place behind the bent-over blonde, eyeing the inviting ass with pleasure, I beckoned the fair Iryna to me. She came with her usual indifference, and let me take her by the hand. With just the slightest trace of reticence, the lissome blonde allowed herself to be drawn down to lay across my wide spread thighs. She shifted her hips to rest more comfortably, her long, lean body fully stretched out over my lap, hip pressed against my hard penis, the shimmering hair sweeping down to floor on one side while her slender legs angled down so the toes touched the floor on the other. I sighed in deep admiration of the sleek ass she presented to me, that choice upturned bottom, two taut, elongated ovals that simply begged to be caressed . . . or spanked!

I fitted my curved hand to those tight, little mounds and moved it slowly, absently stroking the girl's rearend, up and down those delectable twin curves while I turned my attention to Helva's punishment. Minta had taken up her position, careful to stand to one side so that she would not block my view of Helva's handsome bottom, the mounds stretched taut, offered up so nicely. I watched the wiry girl tighten her grip, and slowly draw back the wooden paddle. She brought her weapon down with surprising force in one smooth, well-aimed swing.

THWAP!

The resounding slap of the pliant wood blade as it met the padded flesh of Helva's meaty behind was reassuringly solid; the girl's shoulders jerked as she took the full shock of the impact. Minta's smile widened, and I noticed an excited gleam in her eyes as she widened her stance, and brought back the paddle, eager to deliver the next smack.

THWAP! THWAP! . . . THWAP! THWAP! THWAP! The punishing paddle bit into the vulnerable rearmounds with a dull, thudding regularity, sending the big girl squirming furiously, twisting her loins in a futile effort to escape the business-like walloping. Loud vehement braying sounds were coming from around the gag as Helva shrieked her outrage.

Watching Helva's spanking soon had my rock-hard prick throbbing with the ache of desire. I dipped a hand between Iryna's loose thighs and avidly explored the mysteries I found there, shamelessly fingering her sex while she writhed helplessly in my lap. I took her cuntlips between my fingers, feeling her heat, and sampling the slick wetness of her pussy. Iryna moaned softly while my fingers played with the soft folds of her rapidly moistening cunt.

Now Minta was toying with her victim, pausing to study the reddened throbbing cheeks, running the wooden blade up and over the swelling domes, tapping them ever so lightly just to see the cheeks clench in fear.

I was by now wildly excited; my eager hands greedily fondling Iryna's firm young loins. Minta was waiting for just the right moment, and when she saw the tense mounds slacken, she hauled back to deliver a decisive smack, . . . followed swiftly by another, and another.

THWAP! THWAP! THWAP! THWAP!

The continuing thud of the wood splattering those fleshy mounds, the sight of the wiry slave spanking the big blonde, heating her ass till she mewed loudly and wriggled in frantic gyrations—it all drove me wild. I fitted my hand to the sweet curvature of Iryna's tempting little butt and squeezed, digging my fingers into the meaty mounds, kneading those small cheeks till I had my slave girl twitching uncontrollably and whimpering with passion. I kept my eyes on the captivating scene before me, while I began spanking the writhing girl in my lap, lightly smacking her taut little butt, pausing to caress the blushing mounds with the cupped palm of my hand, then laying on more crisp smacks. Thoroughly enjoying myself, I kept alternating between these two approaches, caressing her ass, and punishing her ass, teasing the lithe blonde with mixed feelings till I got a soft moan of pleasure from her inverted head. A shiver of desire rippled through her shoulders, followed by a hot little wiggle of the hips that told me this shy, quiet girl was undoubtedly aroused, energized by the masculine hand that warmed her bottom.

Minta had paused once again and stood with hands on hips, admiring the angry pink blush that had formed across the smiling under curves of Helva's shapely ass. Her thin smile widened into a truly evil grin as she saw her former mistress work her butt muscles, the mounds clenching, as she tried desperately to harden herself to receive the next punishing slap from her former slave. The poised butt was tense, the skin taut, the sides hollowed out, and the crack reduced to a narrowed slit, as her victim held herself fearfully, waiting. Minta also waited, letting the anticipation build, and then she struck, whacking those hardened rearcheeks with a glancing slap topped off by an extra snap of the wrist.

THWAP!

Now she settled into a smooth, easy rhythm, spanking her victim, not terribly hard but crisp and methodically, pulling her hand back only halfway, but giving a little snap to the wrist as the wooden blade bit into the cringing mounds, and the blonde threw back her head and brayed her protest into her gag.

The little slave seemed a crazed woman, eagerly delivering those short choppy smacks, alternating her attack from one cheek to the other, precisely whacking each rearcheek of the hot, squirming behind. I was fascinated by Minta's expression. As she watched the wobbly mounds dancing under her relentless slaps, her eyes narrowed into gleaming slits. Her lips were drawn back, her jaw was set as she gleefully attacked the older girl's agitated rearend, spanking with maniacal fury. Muffled grunts, at first interspersed with the solid thunk of the wooden paddle splattering the fleshy mounds, quickly became continuous, escalating into high-pitched keening cries, effectively muffled, but shrilly insistent cries of protest, as all the while Helva twisted in anguish.

I was walloping Iryna's ass hard now, thoroughly enjoying spanking her, while she yelped and kicked up her heels, twisting excitedly in my lap. I relished the feel of the girl's heaving loins as she bounded up and down in my lap to the steady rhythm of my smacking hand. As she writhed in fiery agitation, her naked haunches pressed against my upright prick sending a deep shudder of pleasure through me. Before I realized what was happening, there was a startling surge of ecstatic delight, and I was . . . coming, my seed spewing forth in thick creamy spurts that shot up into the air to rain down on Iryna's delightfully bouncy ass.

Chapter Ten

A SLAVE OF ROME

The next few days I spent in leisure, testing out my new slave girls in various ways, taking all three in every conceivable manner. Minta was proving to be a real find: a pure sex kitten, endlessly inventive, boldly seductive, and positively reveling in lusty decadence. There was nothing this fun-loving, spirited, young vixen wouldn't try. The girl's appetite was insatiable! Cool Iryna still retained much of her Northern reserve, but she was gradually thawing out and becoming more pliant. She still showed little enthusiasm for her new role, and her passivity continued to irritate me, but at least she would obey. Helva, on the other had, refused to accept her subjugation. She did nothing without being forced to, and then she performed only grudgingly. In spite of the blistering her ass had taken at the hands of the vengeful-minded Minta, she remained an unruly and obdurate slave. When I took her, it was like fucking a board. Her hard silent eyes seemed to say: "You might have my body, but you will find no pleasure in it." I found her haughty insolence a bold challenge, and I resolved to conquer this proud beauty till I had her raging in sensual lust and begging to be fucked.

Naturally, I sought Kimar's advice. He stood regarding the two recalcitrant slaves as they knelt together before us. Minta, her hard young body dimly visible in her sheer tunic, was attending us, serving wine, and just being available. I watched her bend over to pour the wine, and studied her straight boyish butt, while I waited for my guest to offer an opinion. Kimar let his shrewd experienced gaze pass over the merchandise, for that is how he saw all slaves. Summoning them to approach on their knees, he took his time conducting a critical examination of the naked bodies of the two blond women, evaluating them only with his eyes, for he never touched them, and would not without asking my permission first, for that would hardly be polite. But as much as he might desire to run his hands over those splendid blond bodies, there was no need. He had inspected thousands of slaves in his time, but I could tell he was impressed with these exquisite possessions of mine. His face held a thoughtful expression when, at last, he turned to me.

"I have a suggestion Marcus," he began decisively. "As you know I have certain methods that have proven useful in training slaves. Why not turn them over to me for a while, say three or four days, a week perhaps; no more will be needed. In no time, I will have these fillies straining at the traces in a spirited chariot race, where, I'll wager they'll make a good show of themselves. I can promise that when I deliver them back to you, you will not be able to find more compliant and willing sex slaves anywhere in the Empire! Once I am through with them, these women will jump to carry out your every wish; they will obey with alacrity and unbounded enthusiasm."

It was an offer I couldn't refuse. And so it came about that I gave the girls to Kimar. The next day two of his henchmen showed up to take them in hand. With hands tied behind them, ankles loosely hobbled, they were led by leashes attached to their collars, drawn along to stumble after their handlers on their way to the camp of the master slaver.

———✖———

True to his word, it was exactly one week later that Kimar had arranged a sort of bacchanal to which I was invited, along with a handful of select guests. Stripped to nothing but loincloths, we lounged about on fine velvet couches, while before us tables set with silver dishes were piled high with rich and exotic foods. The robust wine flowed freely, and it was pleasing to find that one's slightest needs were instantly attended to by a bevy of comely slave girls, whose naked presence amongst us helped to add to the simmering sense of excitement, the growing anticipation as we eagerly awaited the appearance of the stars of the evening—my two blond slaves, about whom the guests had heard much, and were now most keen to see.

Eventually, Kimar gave the long-awaited order and a pair of slaves threw back the flaps of the big tent to treat us to a most astonishing sight! An overseer stood in the entranceway, a big stocky fellow who stood with legs boldly spread, bare-chested, and otherwise naked but for the leather thongs of sandals that snaked up his muscular calves, and a brief kilt of animal skins slung low on his sturdy hips. His left hand, hanging loosely at his side, idly fingered the handle of a leather paddle, while wrapped around his right hand was a rawhide leash. At the other end of the leash was the collared throat of a stunning blond slave girl! She knelt beside him, hands at her sides, sitting back on her haunches, her blond head bowed in docile submission. An awed hush came over the raunchy crowd.

At his curt command, the girl was drawn up onto hands and knees, and forced to crawl after her handler as he boldly swaggered into the tent. I thrilled to see Helva, my proud Nordic beauty, thus subjugated, forced to adopt this humiliating posture, made to crawl naked, like some big blond beast, before Kimar's wide-eyed guests. As the pair entered, we now saw that a second overseer was standing partially hidden in the shadows behind the first. He too, held the leash of a blond slave, a slender young woman whose sleek body moved like a large cat's, her narrow butt swaying from side to side as she strove to keep up with her striding handler. We watched in silence while this little procession made its circuit in front of the open circle of couches upon which reclined Kimar's ogling guests.

My elegant beauty crawled with her head hung low and her handler, noticing her poor posture, snapped a crisp command. When she didn't comply quickly enough to suit him, the wicked paddle shot out to slap her churning cheeks with a sharp retort that had her instantly jerk up her head, to continue crawling with chin raised, face forward, as he had ordered to do. The girls were paraded back and forth before us while we let our eyes feast on the delightful display. Their blond manes had been fixed identically, combed into long silken strands, pulled back from their pale faces, and tied into lengths of lank pony-tails.

The big blonde moved with animal grace, her flanks flowing with rippling muscles, her rearcheeks shifting most seductively. I admired the smooth clean narrow lines of Iryna's nude form as she crawled by, her straight hipless flanks swaying liquidly, small buttocks moving in provocative rhythm. As she came closer I observed a very thin golden chain encircling her waist. From this chain a single, gold thread hung down the back to disappear between her shifting cheeks, as it passed between her legs. I saw that the fine links were embedded in the bulging fig of her vulva that peeked out at us from between her moving thighs. Apparently, the narrow chain had been drawn up between the cuntlips, to continue its way up in front where it bisected the girl's blond vulva before meeting the center of the waist chain. I saw both slave's bodies were adorned with identical gold chains tightly encircling their slim waists just above their hips. It crossed my mind that the slaves must have hated to wear such a chain pulled so taut that it bit into the softness of their hidden clefts, the embedded links chafing the tender labia as they moved. Perhaps it was that irritant that accounted for the occasional wince of distress I saw pass over their pale brows as they crawled before us. But I only knew the half of it!

After several laps of being paraded around before those appreciative connoisseurs, Kimar clapped his hands and the handlers drew their charges up till they faced us, side by side, still on hands and knees. From this front view, with their heads raised well up, it was possible to see each girl's breasts beneath her lithe torso—Helva's breasts formed into two tit-bags that hung soft and inviting, with thick tips pointed straight down; Iryna's small globes, drawn by gravity to hang in full pendulous shapes, swayed succulently beneath her bent torso.

Now, at a word from the master slaver, the leashes were jerked and the girls straightened up to sit back on their haunches while the leashes were untied from their banded necks. They made a delightful pair, kneeling there side by side: the classic Nordic beauty in the full flower of mature womanhood, the silvery blond hair, the full firm curves of those proud breasts so openly displayed; and the slighter version beside her, the hair a pure white yellow, like summer hay, the gently sloping shoulders of that lithe willowy form with its small understated tits that perched before us with such enticingly audacious nipples. The slave girls held the pose for a moment or two till, at the nod of the master slaver, they fell forward, crouching down on their elbows, and then bowing down so low that they touched their foreheads to the rug.

They held that pose for a long mesmerizing interval and then, continuing what had obviously become a well-practiced routine, they rose to their feet as one and turned in place, so that they stood with their backs to us. Without a word of command, the obedient slaves fell to their knees once again, pressing their foreheads to the rug in humble subservience, while promptly offering up their pretty behinds for our approval. One of the handlers muttered something, and the two girls shifted a bit, pulling their knees up under them and arching their backs in even deeper curves, thus raising their bottoms so that those appealing buttocks jutted back at us in lewd presentation.

"You see before you a pair of well-trained slaves," Kimar began proudly, speaking to his guests while keeping his eyes on the uplifted feminine behinds that patiently waited to be of service. "They have been taught to obey. They have learned how to be good little slaves. They have learned to crawl on hands and knees, at command, buttocks up and forehead to the ground; and in that way to present themselves for mounting should their master wish to take them in that manner."

He now moved closer to Helva's outthrust buttocks. "And lest they should lapse, we have given each certain reminders of her place: The neck encircled with the high stiff collar, wrist and ankles banded, and oh yes, one further reminder, one the slave cannot see but one whose presence will be sorely felt, a minor irritant perhaps, yet one that will keep her constantly aware of her subservient status."

He placed a confident hand on the tautly-drawn domes of Helva's upturned rump, patted her lightly, affectionately, then slipped his fingers under the delicate chain, following it to where it was lodged deep between the girl's buttocks. Prying open the shapely hemispheres, he revealed that the chain passed through the eye of a rounded butt-plug, drawn tight so that it held the anal intruder securely in place.

"The slave will wear these chains while going about her ordinary household duties during the day, and for other duties at night as well. They can, of course, be easily removed should the master wish to take his slave in that particular place."

So saying he proceeded to demonstrate by detaching the chain and pulling it from between her legs. Now as he held the straining cheeks apart, he dug his fingers into the soft flesh around the flanged end of the ivory plug causing the girl's hips to squirm uneasily. He began to draw out the plug, slowly extracting it as the distended anus seemed to cling to the ivory shaft as it emerged to reveal that it bore the shape of a long, smooth phallus, thin and tapering.

Almost the entire length of the ivory phallus had emerged when Kimar noticed the little agitated wiggle that passed through the girl's rump. A thin smile curled the edge of his lips, as he viciously twisted his hand, screwing the rod deeper into his impaled victim who gave out with a tight-lipped grunt and kicked up her heels at the suddenness of this unexpected violation. For a moment, the master slaver played with the slave, diddling the girl's ass for our amusement, jiggling the wicked intruder that was once more lodged well up the squirming bottom, while she writhed in silent agitation. He toyed with the blond girl a bit more, moving the shaft in and out, till finally, tiring of the game, he withdrew the long thin rod, getting a moan of relief from the upended slave. Kimar laughed, and gave the rebounding cheeks a lusty slap as he watched them snap shut, and clamp down tight.

"We use a lotion to ease the way during insertion," he explained. "You should have seen them move their tails when we mixed a bit of hot spices with the lubricant," he chuckled, turning his back on the salaaming woman.

Now, he moved over to Iryna and stood contemplating her uplifted behind for a long moment. He couldn't help running a hand up and over the twin mounds. Her little "reminder," he told us, would be left in place, cozily ensconced up her rectum. She would have additional restraints applied, for her role would be to attend to the guests, while a special treat was being arranged for her cohort. At his order, the two young women were released from the subservient pose they held and allowed to resume their previous position, kneeling, sitting back on their heels.

A nod from Kimar, brought his assistants who came forth to prepare Iryna for her duties. First she was gagged. I knew from experience that Iryna hated the gag, and yet she now docilely accepted the wadded silk they stuffed in her open mouth. The wide band of leather pressed against her teeth, keeping the wad in place. The ends of the strap were tied together behind her head, imprisoning her soft blond hair. The two men worked quickly and efficiently. They had done this sort of thing many times before. Next, the girl's hands were drawn before her and the cuffs attached to one another by a thin chain of gold. Finally, a length of chain was used to couple her ankle bands in a similar fashion. Shackled like a slave, although with light golden chains, she would be forced to shuffle along, her movements hampered, yet left free enough to allow her to perform her duties if she were careful, all the while being constantly made aware of her servile status. Meanwhile the rude intruder remained in that hidden place, lodged well up her behind so that, as she performed her serving duties, every movement would remind her of certain other obligations she might be called upon to fulfill at the whim of her master.

Now I had her fetch the wine and smiled as she brought the jug, shuffling with an oddly comical gait. Beckoning her closer I held out my cup and as she bent down to pour the wine I couldn't resist reaching up to finger a dangling tit, the soft satiny smooth flesh of the small, soft, globular pendant that hung so temptingly before me. Urging her a step closer, I had her bring the hanging succulent tit-bag down to my open mouth so I could draw in the dangling nipple between my lips and suckle on her while I ran a hand up and down her haunches and felt up her trim rearend.

This delightful dalliance brought my manhood to rigid attention and I dismissed her with a friendly smack on the tail, sending her off to see to the other guests, while I turned my attention back to Helva who knelt quietly before us.

My beauty knelt with chin held high and eyes straight forward, and as my gaze fell to her breasts, I noticed that the girl's nipples had become erected, the hard points protruding out from the taut expanded aureoles! Out of the corner of her eye she noticed me looking at her, and as she turned every so slightly, I was sure I saw a trace of a secretly seductive smile. Astonished, I smiled back and saw her eyes drop to my crotch and the tip of her tongue emerge to quickly rim her lips. There was a surprising eagerness there, a definite gleam in her eye that I had never seen before. I saw a twitch run through her shoulders and her thighs clenched as she rubbed them together in a tiny movement no one else could observe.

Now, the big blonde was ordered to her feet, so that she might take her place under a wooden frame that had been erected at one end of the tent: A wide crossbar supported by two sturdy columns and from which four evenly-spaced ropes hung down. The slave girl scrambled to her feet, eager to take her place, and without being told to, flung herself down on the rug, enthusiastically offering herself up for a sexual ordeal, the very thought of which seemed to get her juices flowing. I noticed this new spirit of cooperation in the way she helped, as the men prepared her. She moved without being told, willingly extending her limbs, freely offering them the cuffs, all the while biting her lower lip as if in keen anticipation. The transformation was remarkable, and had it been simply the results of Kimar's training it would have been truly astonishing. But I later leaned that this new-found desire to please sexually, had been abetted by a secret potion that the old slaver sometimes used to heighten the sexual awareness of his sex slaves, an elixir that turned them into wild lust-driven animals.

It was obvious to me that the girl was already excited as she sprawled impatiently on her back, her pointy nipples sticking straight up. She lay spread-eagled on the floor, while her wrist and ankle bands were being attached to the ends of the four ropes that hung from the high crossbeam. She was not gagged, for Kimar wanted her to be able to use her mouth to pleasure as many guests as possible. With her limbs properly secured, they began to tighten the ropes raising her outstretched body till she swung suspended from the sturdy crossbar. The ropes on her ankles were raised slightly more than those of holding her wrists so that her loins were up-tilted. In this vulnerable position her legs were widespread, her body slightly bowed, slung only a few feet above the grounds, so that by stepping between the outstretched legs, one would have ready access to her gaping cunt.

She raised her head up to look at us from between her widespread legs, and the face I saw was that of a woman in heat. Her lips moved nervously as though in a silent mumble, and her eyes were hard with a bright gleam of lust. Even now, there was a trace of wetness that appeared on the tiny blond curls, edging the ragged lips of her open pussy.

Now Kimar ordered that a chair be brought for me, and had it placed just beyond the girl's hanging feet directly opposite her sex, so that my view was down along the converging lines her legs made to the open vertex. From my vantage point I could see the thin haze of pubic hair that shaded into a cloudy tuft on the crest of her mounded vulva and spilled down between her legs where the tiny wisps of pussyhair ridged her gaping pink cleft. Initially, he wished me only to observe, to watch my blond beauty's reactions as she eagerly took on three of Kimar's guests, who had readily volunteered for duty. Quintus peeled off his loin-cloth and stationed himself behind her so that once her inverted head was allowed to hang freely down, her mouth would be readily available to his swollen cock. At either side two more naked men, Decimus and Valerius, took up their positions, standing so that their upright cocks were placed just beyond the grasp of the girl's straining fingers.

Her tall, blond body hung open and vulnerable, the ragged rising and falling of her breasts attesting to her growing excitement as she waited with eyes closed, breathing through parted lips. She made a breathtaking pic-ture stretched out as she was, her sleek lines bowed, her feminine charms brazenly exposed; arms stretched over-head; the strain in her sagging body was quite evident in the taut sinews of her long arms and tapering thighs. Her mounded breasts were slightly flattened, while her upstanding nipples stood fully erect, the tiny protruding nubs, staunchly distended, protruded stiffly with anticipa-tory excitement, a blatant testament to her tingling state of arousal.

A jar of oil was brought to them, and the men oiled their hands and then coated their upright cocks. Helva twisted from side to side, and I saw her lick her lips at the sight of the well-oiled cocks that stood upright, gleaming in their eagerness just inches from the reach of her fingers. Her fists clenched in frustration, as her wrists pulled on their tethering lines. I soon saw that in this configuration, her hands and mouth would be usefully employed, and only her open cunt remained free and available; *that* passage had been reserved for me!

Now, they proceeded to coat her body with oil, beginning with her hands that clenched in reflex at the tickling of the palms. They passed over the cuffs and rubbed the oily sheen along her sinewy arms and into the softness of her underarms. The blonde twitched excitedly, as they continued on down her curving sides, over the delicate traces of her ribcage and along her flanks to cross over her hips and tease into the crease at her belly. They were careful to work together, keeping pace with one another, as they glided up her front, while her torso shook and trembled. Her head was up and she was watching their progress through slitted eyes, but she let it fall weakly back as she gave her body up to the slippery hands that by now had found the flattened mounds of her firm, young tits.

They thoroughly enjoyed those superb breasts, coating them with a thin sheen of oil; Decimus massaging, pulling and stretching the pliant flesh of her left breast, while Valerius fondled, and played lavishly with the right one. Their hands soon had her burning with lust as the highly-agitated blonde clenched her eyes shut tight against the rising tide of arousal and shook her head from side to side, mumbling incoherently in her strange foreign tongue. They tweaked her stiff nipples, rolling them between thumb and forefinger, pulling on those aching tips, while the passion-driven female squirmed sensuously, twisting her shoulders in maddened desire as they mercilessly teased her, toyed with her, playing with her oily tits, fondling her mounds lavishly, till they had her mumbling and whimpering for more.

When it became evident that the slave girl was fully aroused by this tit play, her two admirers perversely quit her heaving breasts, only to move on down over her belly, across to the cradle of her hanging hips, around the curve, and up her sleek haunches, then circling around the nicely-rounded thighs as the inner sinews twitched at the intimate touch. In this way they explored every inch of that lovely sagging body, but for the place right between the splayed legs, for when their hands neared her womanhood, Kimar beckoned me forward.

I jumped up with cock fully erect and stepped eagerly between the vee of the hanging girl's legs. Brushing the pads of my fingers through the silken hairs and then more firmly, palming her pubis, brought a sharp hiss of breath as the tense female quivered with anticipation. I crooked two fingers and slid them quite easily right up her glistening cunt, to feel her slick pussylips, well-moistened by now with the free flow of feminine juices. She gurgled as I thrust up into her. She might have come right then and there, with the slightest jiggling of my probing hand, but we would not grant her such imme-diate relief. Withdrawing my glistening fingers, I poured some oil into my palm, then cupped her vulva and palmed her, soaking the tiny curls with oil, rubbing it into the soft folds of her pussy. Helva let out a purr which rose into a long, wavering moan as I curved my fingers, fitting my palm to her damp, hot sex so I could clamp her soft cunt tightly in my hand.

My firm fondling of her most private parts soon had our blond sex slave writhing uncontrollably, thrashing about in her bounds and clenching her jaws. Her hips bucked, while a series of deep staccato grunts escaped her tightened lips. The girl was fully aroused now, burning with erotic frenzy, her healthy young body resonating to the repeated sexual thrills she was forced to endure as the delicious feel of those warm masculine hands moved all over her body, firing her lust to a fevered pitch. Suddenly, she began whipping her head from side to side in a demented fury; the long silky strands flung wildly about. Her groans were more open now, deepening into low, earthy, shivering moans, then becoming filled with urgency, groans interspersed with foreign words that tumbled out in a heated rush, incomprehensible, but desperate pleas for release from the unremitting stimulation of our pleasuring hands. Abruptly, her bounding hips came up, and she held herself there, stretching out her sleek-muscled limbs to the limits for the longest possible moment of ecstasy, before she exploded in a furious bucking, her wild and frantic gyrations yanking on her bounds, uncaring, as a long, plaintive cry escaped her lips.

Her violent reaction, fired my lust and I attacked her vulnerable pussy, fondling her mercilessly, while my two cohorts grabbed her tits, firmly massaging the slick mounds. Helva shrieked and hollered for us to fuck her in guttural German, and again in Latin, for those were a few of the words she had learned. With a cry of sheer ecstasy, the big blonde threw back her head and came with a mighty climax. Her body was racked with a huge shudder, followed by spastic contractions which yanked at the taut lines suspending her in space. Then she collapsed, and lay slack, sagging, her breasts moving in great gulping heaves. A shiver of aftershock ran through her depleted body; her moans became softer as she slipped into the warmth of a delightful afterglow.

She lay peaceably now, eyes closed, features calm, her slack body perfectly still except for the movement of her gradually subsiding breasts. But she was not to be permitted to rest for long; not at least, while masculine needs were left unattended.

Accordingly, we each stepped forward. Decimus and Valerius, their rock-hard pricks swaying in the air, each took a hand and placed them on their aroused manhood, so that she held them both by their cocks. Meanwhile, Quintus who stood at her head and had, until now, taken no part in the proceedings, beyond occasionally slipping his fingers through the long blond hair, now placed his hands on the sides of her face and pulled her head till it tilted backward. Helva hung with head inverted, and when her eyes fluttered open, she found herself staring directly at Quintus' rigid cock which stood at rigid attention just inches from her face. For a moment she seemed dazed, uncomprehending, but Quintus gave the groggy girl no time to adjust to the situation, preferring instead to rub his prick on her face, and press the head demandingly against her open lips.

She licked her lips and opened her mouth straining upwards to take his turgid shaft. Quintus allowed her to draw it in between her lips, and pull on him, sucking his shaft into the warmth of her receptive mouth. He grunted, tight-lipped, and let her work him over as he grabbed a handful of silken hair, and drew her head down on him. Holding her face between his hands he moved his hips and proceed to fuck the mouth of that pretty, inverted, blond face.

From the dreamy expression that crossed his countenance you could tell that he found the girl to have a lively and talented tongue. As she sucked off Quintus, the insatiable sex slave gripped the other two men, and holding on tightly, began to jerk them off, pumping her fists with frenzied determination.

With a ragged cry, Decimus threw his head back and abruptly pulled free of her grasp. Grabbing his throbbing prick he held it aimed at her tits, while Valerius followed suite, erupting to send spurting gobs of semen onto her chest and belly. Helva, once again swept up in the grip of passion, tossed her head from side to side and moaned as their seed rained down on her thrashing body. Her second orgasm was smaller and sharper than the first: a brief quivering, punctuated with a sharp yelp of delight. And then she lay still, all the tension drained from her sagging body. And I saw a look as I had never seen on Helva's attractive blond features—the unmistakable smile of sexual satisfaction.

Meanwhile I had my hand between her splayed legs and was slowly massaging the soft folds of her damp sex. I studied the bedraggled figure hanging limply before me. Her hair was soaked; her warm face bathed in sweat. It ran down her chest mingling with the oily lubricant which covered her body in a golden sheen. The highly-charged sexual performance had depleted the girl, but I was still at the height of arousal, burning with feverish lust, fired with a deep rutting need to lay into that throbbing wet cunt.

My cock was aching with lust as, burning with impatience, I clamped my hand on her hot, damp womanhood. The spent female stirred and whimpered, her lips worked as she mumbled something I didn't understand. It made no difference. Stepping up to bring my hips near to her hanging loins, I squatted a little till the crown of my prick came into contact with her cuntlips. I rubbed the swollen head along the slick protruding lips, while the sex-soaked woman whimpered and moaned.

With a rush of wild excitement, I bounded up on my toes, driving straight up into her in a single lusty thrust. The low slung female groaned at the abruptness of the vicious stab, a low earthy rumble trailing out from deep in her throat as I plunged in all the way, and held myself in her warm churning depths.

I waggled my hips, tickling her innards. With a little cock action I soon had Helva whimpering like a hurt puppy. Then I started to move more decisively, thrusting into her slick juicy cunt, fucking her with slow deeply-penetrating strokes. The ravaged female, rolled her head and stirred to life; her hips started twitching as the simmering passion fires were re-awakened once more.

Now I was fucking her with gusto, pumping with a steady rhythm, a lusty, jolting tempo that had her writhing uncontrollably. Once again, she was swept up, driven towards the peak of yet another climax. Moaning in a guttural growl she urged me on, her hips bucking up to meet mine. Maddened with lust, I pounded into her, furiously fucking her with wild abandon while she swung crazily in her sling. The frenzied female was oblivious now, rolling her head from side to side, mumbling incoherently in feverish whispers, then yelling out, calling on her strange gods and cursing me in her foreign tongue, but always, unmistakably, urging me on and on. Finally, she let out a long desperate groan as an all-consuming rapture lifted her up and swept her along towards a third shattering orgasm.

She came this time with a plaintive cry, cut short by a

mighty shudder that racked her slender frame. A single intense thrill of pure pleasure shot through me as, with a final powerful lunge, I fired my load into her throbbing depths, flooding her innards with pulsating jets of creamy sperm, till I tumbled down the other side of my climax.

My knees weakened, and I collapsed against Helva's hanging body, draping myself over her, savoring the feel of her sweating, oily flesh as I lay with my chest pressed against those warm slippery breasts. Thoroughly depleted, I lay there, plastered to her hot slick body, closing my eyes to let the blissful peace of a warm afterglow flood through me.

The shrewd slaver saw immediately the wave of excitement the introduction of these rare blond slaves would cause in decadent Rome. In no time Teutons would be all the rage, and the elite of society simply have to own one, or even a half dozen to grace their elegant homes. He knew that the Nordic women would be especially prized and that he could demand, and get, outrageous fees for them. He looked at me very earnestly when he said, in a voice of solemn promise: "We need more of them, and if you can supply me with them, I can make you a rich man."

As it turned out, there were continued eruptions among the Northern tribes, as though in answer to Kimar's prayers. Over the next few months the gods were with us, and our frequent campaigning yielded several caches of these magnificent barbarians. Kimar was as good as his promise, so that when I was finally called back to Rome, it would be as a very wealthy man indeed.

And so I was to enter the imperial city at the head of my bevy of fair-haired slaves, rich, successful, and influential beyond my wildest dreams, to find myself eagerly embraced by the cream of Roman society. I was even summoned to the presence of the Emperor himself, extended a prized invitation to an orgy at the imperial palace. To this event, I would bring Helva, the wild barbarian of the North, who I knew would create quite a stir when she appeared at that decadent court.

Among the nobly outfitted courtiers and their elegantly dressed ladies, she would stand out, stark naked, wearing nothing but the collar of a slave of Rome—and she would wear it proudly! She would be paraded before them, unable to avoid the lusty hunger in their eyes as they appraised her splendid nude body; and with some of her fellow slaves, she might be made to perform at the whim of the Emperor, and the world's most decadent court. Only then would she fully realize her abject subjugation, the extent of the humiliation she must endure. She would truly understand only at the moment when she was forced to enter the grand hall on her hands and knees, crawling like an animal to make her humble obeisance, and lowering her head to touch the marble floor before the mighty Emperor of Rome.

The End

ROMANS!
A PONYGIRLS TALE

Author's Note: Every writer of erotic fiction should try at least one ponygirl story. This is mine.

—D.W.

With the successful conclusion of our spring campaign, the Bernesium garrison was ordered to stand down and immediately retire back to our barracks. We were relieved in more ways than one; thanking the gods to be alive and more or less intact. We were all looking forward to a well-deserved rest. The Germanic hordes had finally been beaten back, at least for now. Of course, we knew it would be so. It was just a matter of time. No people on earth could stand against the power of Rome, once the decision was made to unleash the legions against them. It was a familiar story: barbarian tribes rebelling, then steadily, methodically pounded into submission, one after the other.

And so with a summer of peace before us, army life settled into its usual dull routine. And if things lacked excitement at our little outpost on the northern fringe of the world's mightiest empire, well, at least there was no shrieking mob of dirty, foul-smelling savages trying their best to get at you with the intention of lopping off your head! All in all, peace is so much more desirable than war—even if it does make army life a bit boring.

Truth be told, there was not much to do at Bernesium. Between visits to the Gratius' whores, Lucius and I spent most of our time at Filo's, one of two local taverns, gambling, wrenching, and solving all the problems of the Empire. With the aid of the heady local wine, our problem-solving went on till the wee small hours of the morning.

The room was warm; the crowd lively and raucous. Lucius, in his cups, was at that point in the evening when he was loudly swearing to all around us, that he and I were the best of eternal comrades, brothers in arms. With one arm slung around my shoulder, he closed in on me, breathing his wine-saturated breath in my face, while filling my cup with the other hand.

"Marcus, my friend, you must come with me to the parade grounds on Thor's day. The word is Kimar intends to exercise his slaves in one of his famous chariot races—*that* is something you will not want to miss."

I had heard of these extravaganzas from old-timers at the post, but I knew them only by reputation, since no such games had been held since my posting to Bernesium.

Those were the days when Rome seemed to need an endless supply of fresh slaves, and the slave traffic, in spite of bandits, hijackers, and savage tribes, was very lucrative indeed! The slave caravans normally bypassed us preferring a more easterly route, but it so happened that during my tour of duty at Bernesium, they were diverted to the north by one of those frequent dustups with the quarrelsome Scythians.

It was our good luck that slavers choosing this northern route would seek safe haven in Bernesium after the long and dangerous hardships of their mountain crossing. Under the shelter of our garrison, they could rest their drivers and their precious human cargo, and replenish their supplies before pushing on to the eternal city. And so it was that one of the wealthiest and most renown slavers of all, a crafty worthy by the name of Kimar, arrived with his caravan and was now encamped on the grassy plains just outside the walls of the town.

It was a pleasant June day, warm with a slight breeze. A festive crowd of soldiers, farmers, and town's people had gathered to watch the various games which pitted slave against slave in athletic competitions. The crowd delighted in seeing athletic young slaves, their healthy naked bodies straining and sweating in the sun, as they were put through their paces by burly slave drivers. But these games were only preliminary events for the highlight of the day—the chariot races in which slaves girls would be enlisted as ponygirls, with "red" and "blue" teams competing for the honors. Of course, the racing "chariots" were hardly the heavy armored war chariots such used by the legions, but rather specially made lightweight traps, nothing more than a delicate frame of saplings mounted on two spindly wheels.

As the time for the races approached the crowds began to gather around the track, an oval of beaten earth from where they might cheer on their favorites. The reason for the popularity of Kimar's races was well-known: he specialized in the most exquisite sex slaves, beautiful girls and pretty boys kept naked but for their high collars and the leather straps that banded wrist and ankles. These lovely creatures were far too valuable to serve as common domestics, or as laborers in the fields. No, their labors would be of a very different nature, performed in the bedchambers of Rome's elite.

Lucius and I plunged into the crowd. People here quickly stepped aside for a Roman officer out of respect and the high esteem in which we were held. One of the benefits of service in such an isolated outpost is that officers, even minor ones such as ourselves were treated with a respect and deference the mobs of Rome would never show to a junior officer. We made our way to the platform that had been set up under a canopy. Nearby, stood the tent where the ponygirls were being readied. Cushioned seats had been provided for the various dignitaries with whom the old slaver meant to curry favor. We took our places besides the handful of minor officials and tradesmen who constituted the local nobility. From our vantage point we could get a clear view of the proceedings, and we watched with interest as the preparations were made for the main event.

Our host now mounted the platform, and proceeded to greet each of his guests. Kimar was a scrawny fellow with big ears and an ingratiating grin, whose bald head bobbed up and down comically as he bowed before each seated dignitary while taking his hand in greeting. The man was a well known ass-kisser, fawning over any Roman he met if he thought the fellow might possibly be of use to him. Now he took his place to one side, waiting for silence like an impresario about to present his production in a premiere performance. He stood there overlooking the mob with surprising dignity, prepared to wait till he got their attention. Kimar was a showman, and this was his supreme moment. Such performances were his way of showing off his slaves. Kimar knew the crowd would be dazzled by their graceful beauty, athletic prowess, and precise discipline, thus adding to his considerable reputation as the purveyor of the finest goods. He clapped his hands twice and the flaps of the tent were drawn back to allow the passage of a parade of six beautiful girls who stepped forward in single file onto the grassy field.

There was a moment of stunned silence, then a murmur of wonder broke out in the crowd: the girl's naked bodies had been dyed, colored from head to foot in the colors of their teams; three ruddy red girls emerged, followed by three whose bodies had been tinged with blue! The crowd broke into wild applause, which our grinning impresario acknowledged with a deep bow of his head.

We saw that each girl wore leather straps banding her arms just above the elbow. Prior to making her entrance, the girl's arms were drawn behind her and these cuffs attached to each other. This enforced a rigid posture with chest arched out and arms well back at their sides as they strode into view. The little parade continued as the contestants passed in review, circling the grassy area in front of our grandstand, walking with heads held high, and breasts proudly displayed.

The red team came first. Red I was a tall, striking beauty, with long shapely legs, whose full, heavy tits rose in flattened mounds that lolled on her proud chest. She possessed the straight blond mane typical of Germanic woman. Red II was thinner, and all but flat-chested. Leaner than Red I, but just as tall, she also one of those Nordic beauties with that typical narrow, sleek body, and hair that formed a helmet of white spun gold. Red III was slightly built, with playful little titties, and a cute, saucy bottom. Her limbs were straight and narrow, and her chestnut hair formed a loose mop cropped short over her youthful features.

Blue I, like the Red leader, was a well-built, long-legged girl. But unlike the northern girls, she had a gorgeous mane of thick dark hair which suggested a southern ancestry. From the dark sensual eyes, large breasts, wide hips and generous bottom, I guessed that she was from one of the Latin tribes. Blue II was lean and hard-bodied with a splay of tawny hair. Spare and athletically built, her tight conical breasts stuck straight out, swaying before her with a certain insolence as she strode by. Blue III, with her close-cropped brown hair, had a tight, compact body. Her firmly rounded tits sported up-tilted nipples. Her strong sinewy legs and robust thighs suggested hidden power.

As each passed by, Lucius and I compared the girl's attributes; a wager was laid. While I thought Red I's tall rangy body and long strides would give her an edge, perhaps a commanding lead in yoke with her red sisters, Lucius was of the opinion that while the leaders were equally strong, the blue supporting team was athletically superior to their red counterparts, and they might well carry the day.

Slaves must be taught to present themselves properly. To demonstrate, the girls now formed a line facing the platform and came to attention before their overlord and his esteemed guests, legs together, heads held high, shoulders squared, hands behind their backs. Their lineup gave us an opportunity to further evaluate their naked bodes. Like all sex slaves, they had been shorn of all body hair. Unlike those who followed the latest trends however, Kimar allowed his slaves to keep the hair on their heads. There were those slave drivers these days, and even quite a few owners whose slaves were completely denuded, or went about with head hair that had been reduced to a fine stubble. But Kimar was a traditionalist: he believed that feminine beauty was enhanced by a girl's crowning glory, so Kimar's girls were allowed to keep their hair.

At a gesture from one of the overseers, the six slaves obediently bowed to the stands, and held the position, bending low from the waist, while the audience applauded. Kimar gave a little wave, the girls straightened, and the overseers came forward to begin the task of preparing the ponygirls.

I was quite taken by the imperious manner of Red I, and watched in fascination as the proud beauty was harnessed up.

One of the handlers, a stocky, bearded fellow in a leather jerkin, approached her with body harness in hand. I admired the way Big Red stuck out her chest, brazenly flaunting her big-nippled breasts for all to see. Well-disciplined, she never flinched an inch as he laid the leather straps on her rigid body.

The groom went about his business methodically. First he buckled on the waist cincher—a wide leather belt that had rings attached at the hips and a narrow strap hanging down from the front. The purpose of the hanging strap was not immediately apparent, but the rings were clearly useful. With the belt in place, the lead girl could be attached to her companions on either side; the belts of the outer girls would be, in turn, attached to the chariot's shafts. I watched as the dour groom tightened the cincher belt, further constricting the tapering waist of the tall red body. Now I saw that a single strap ran up the girl's back to meet a thinner crossing belt that would pass around her body high up under the arms. Once in place, this upper cross-piece was buckled down to loop her upper body just above the breasts.

By this time, all the grooms had set about inspecting the fit, buckling straps, tightening belts, and, of course, taking the opportunity to enjoy themselves by running their hands over the brightly colored bodies of the naked ponygirls to assure a snug fit.

When next I turned my attention to Big Red, her groom had thrown a tangle of straps over her proud head. This turned out to be the head harness, which he was now adjusting into place. A thin band looped the crown of her head, crossing her forehead. From this head band an inverted vee angled down on either side of her nose, to hold a wooden bit that she docilely accepted between her strong white teeth. The last strip ran from ear to ear over the top of her head; the ends, dangling down on either side, were to be gathered under the chin and buckled there. He tightened the chin strap to make sure the head gear fit snugly, imprisoning that blonde mane in straps of leather.

Once all six of those hard young bodies were bound in leather strapping, the ponygirls were led, with straps dangling down between their legs, to their chariots. At the prompting of their overseers, each team stepped into the light wooden frame formed by the shafts and crossbar, and waited, standing hip to hip. At a word of command they reached down simultaneously and picked up the crossbar raising it to hip-level just in front of them.

While their arms remained bound together behind them, there was just enough slack left so that they could bring both hands forward to clasp the crossbar. They would be pushing on the bar while driving forward, keeping their upper bodies erect with shoulders drawn back and chests arched out in front, raising their breasts in proud display.

The chariot's traces were next attached to the harnesses

along their flanks. The grooms now set about attaching the reins to the bridle, and drawing the leather straps back over the ponygirls' shoulders to lay the leads in the seat of the little chariot.

Now we saw that as a further display of the team's colors, each girl was to be supplied with a "tail." These were plumes made of horsehair, dyed in bright red or vibrant blue, and sprouting from squat wooden plugs at one end. Once the plugs were inserted, the plume flopped down limply over the girl's bare bottom. A well-trained ponygirl knew how to swing it by giving a little wiggle as she pranced.

The ponygirls waited in the correct racing posture: chins raised, heads held high, shoulders back, chests stuck out, and most importantly, backs arched so as to present their hindquarters for the whip or, in this case, for the insertion of the tails.

The Red leader stood patiently, ready to accept her tail. She leaned well forward over the waist bar, her rich breasts falling forward to hang heavily under her, while she thrust her rump back in offering. The poor man couldn't help himself. Although it was frowned upon for the hired help to handle the merchandise, he couldn't resist those voluptuous tits.

He grabbed two greedy handfuls and fondled the bending girl lavishly. If having her breasts felt up excited her, you'd never know it, for the well-disciplined girl held the pose without moving a muscle. The groom looked over his shoulder to see that his boss was busy in conversation, and thus emboldened he decided to try for one more bit of fun by sliding a hand down her body to grab an ass cheek, and giving the red girl an affectionate squeeze in a furtive caress that caused her to squirm and wiggle her shoulders. He glanced up to see Kimar looking his way, and quickly gave up his pleasant dalliance to return to work, tugging on the harness, slipping a finger under the straps of buttery leather so as to assure a fit free from slack.

Now we saw the true purpose of the strap that hung from the belt as the groom reached between her legs to take up the strap and pull it through her opened thighs. He drew the strap up between her cheeks and held it taut in her crack while he threaded the end through the slip buckle.

The crotch strap was now deeply embedded between the buttocks, and I noticed that a small metal ring had been set into the strap. This grommet was placed so that, with a bit of adjustment, it ringed the puckered anus. The metal grommet would secure the notched plug, keeping it firmly in place up a girl's ass, throughout even the most strenuous exercise.

The groom left that perfectly-poised ass for just a moment while he coated the little wooden plug with axle grease. Then the stocky fellow planted a beefy hand squarely on Big Red's rump, while the other held the greased plug which he processed to screw up the big girl's churning bottom. Red I wriggled and arched back, jacked upright. Her clenching bottom vigorously squirmed, shaking her newly-acquired tail.

The groom waited for her to settle down before stepping back to call the red team to attention. The three slaves straightened up to assume the proud carriage of well-trained ponygirls at the ready: standing tall, bridled heads held high, breasts thrust out, legs pressed tightly together, clasping the crossbar with both hands. Three bright red tails hung straight down from three tight-cheeked young buttocks.

Once the blue team was similarly prepared and in place, the drivers made their appearance. These were even younger girls; slightly built, light-weight girls being most prized to be trained as jockeys. They were of course naked, their necks were banded with the 4-inch high slave collar. Each was equipped with a thin whippy rod, which, Lucius assured me, they were not reluctant to use. The teams were now lined up, ready for the start of the race.

At an indifferent wave from the preening procurer, a flicking snap of two light whips stung girlish buttocks, and the ponygirls were off to the roar of delight sent up by the enthusiastic crowd.

They began with the ritual of circling the oval at a canter: the two teams in step, side by side. Trained to show off at such performance, they pranced with the sort of classical, high-stepping precision that was much admired among the connoisseurs of such matters: knees raised high, heads thrown back, chin held high, breasts jiggling as they trotted once around the track. After one lap was completed, with the sustained applause of the racing enthusiasts still ringing in their ears, someone banged a drum, and the race was on.

Now the ponygirls broke into a gallop, straining against the bar, legs pistoning furiously, knees pumping high, and bare feet pounding the hardened earth in syncopated rhythm. We watched the well-oiled teams sprint by, eyeing up the bouncy, juddering breasts, and as they passed in front of us, being treated to the sight of six pairs of churning buttocks, adorned with tails that were swishing in time with the jogging rhythm of the running girls, as they retreated down the track. I kept my eye on Big Red, straining mightily, her head back, chest thrust out. Her long-legged stride set the pace, so that her teammates were forced to work even harder to match her, stride for stride.

As they entered the home stretch, the little jockeys began wielding their stinging whips with renewed determination, vigorously slashing at the churning buttocks, while the excited crowd urged on their favorites.

At the end, it was virtually a dead heat, although the red team managed to edge out the blue at the last second. The crowd went wild, and cheers rang out, as the chariots continued circling at a slower pace while the sweating, panting ponygirls struggled for breath, breasts heaving mightily, as they slowed to an easy trot.

Watching the magnificent red leader panting heavily, her long body quivering from the workout, her high-mounded breasts heaving in slowing undulations, I had to reach down to adjust my tunic to ease my stiffened penis. I knew what I had to do!

I Jumped up, pushing my way through the excited crowd to find Kimar. I pulled him aside for a few quick words in an oversized ear. I assured the wily trader that, while he was entitled to a detachment of troops to protect the caravan for the normal 100 leagues from our post, I could personally see to it that he got the very best protection the Roman army could offer. He looked at me suspiciously; narrowed eyes took on a slightly puzzled look. But all he needed was a troop of well-armed soldiers, he countered. Slow on the uptake, I thought. True, I acknowledged, but, I pointed out to him, we had both young, green recruits normally sent on such duties, as well as battle-tested, seasoned veterans. The latter were the kind of stout men who would not turn and run at the first shouts of a thundering horde, leaving a defenseless caravan to the mercies of the wild Germans. And our local Germans *were* an unpredictable lot. They had been acting up lately. With such a valuable cargo as his . . . well, one just never knew . . .

At last, the crafty slave trader saw the light. A sly smile curled his bloodless lips, followed rapidly by a dark scowl. "And the cost of this *extra* service?" he wanted to know. *That* was the question I was a waiting for!

That night, a splendid Nordic beauty was delivered to my quarters. No longer Big Red, she had been rubbed down after the races, bathed and scented, the red dye gone from her statuesque body. And now she knelt before me with eyes downcast, hands behind her back, the golden hair on her bowed head shimmering in the flickering torchlight.

While she was no longer a ponygirl, she presented herself as I had specified: in harness. I wanted for myself the pleasure of relieving her of her bright red tail as she waited on hands and knees for me to mount up. I still have it, nailed up on the wall of my quarters—a piece of tail from a most unforgettable night.

THE RAPE OF THE SABINE WOMEN

Part 1

CALL ME PLUNAR

I am old now. I don't actually feel old, but, I *am* old.

The truth is: for each man, the day comes when the infirmities of age become all too painfully obvious. His once proud sword, no longer responds, as it once did so faithfully, to the call to arms when faced with the plethora of feminine beauty which thrives in our eternal city. My own dance with Eros is no longer a lusty reel, but a pale ballet. At my age, the modest pleasures of watching seem all that the gods have left to me.

Thus I spend hours contemplating the fascinating variations on the feminine form, taking delight in the parade of nude women at the baths, which, like all true Romans, I religiously attend, each and every day.

Ah, to loll peacefully back into the warm scented waters of a heated pool and allow one's eyes to take in each composition of feminine loveliness; naked girls who move with the unpretentious grace of innocent fauns, budding breasts so tentative and pristine; young maidens with small appealing breasts swelling with promise and their nice tight bottoms swaying with a certain charming insouciance. Latin beauties, who lay beside the pools, with languid limbs in repose, managing to seem totally indifferent to the admiring gazes of the young lads who crowd around them, yet are able to bring off the well-time slyly seductive glance with such devastating results. One observes the young bucks, hopelessly smitten, mildly embarrassed to be so helplessly sporting the swelling erections that grow and stiffen at the least provocation. Ah, to be young again!

Then there are the more mature women: wives and mothers, strong, handsome, true Roman matrons with rich backsides, robust thighs, and fulsome breasts; bosoms that they display proudly naked, juddering with the most delightful wobble as they take the few dainty steps to stick a toe into the welcoming waters.

As the reader can see, one can easily wile away many pleasant hours in this manner while reflecting on a life time of what some of our more virtuous brethren would call— overindulgence.

No longer a combatant in the sex wars, I am able to spend my free time in more scholarly pursuits. Between my time at the baths, leisurely meals at some rich man's table (although those invitations I fear are becoming less frequent, for mere scribes are no longer prized as dinner guests as we once were), and afternoon naps under the olive trees in the pleasant shaded atrium of my modest villa, I am engaged in writing what will be, I am sure, the true history of our beloved Rome.

Oh, I know what's going through the reader's mind: Livy. Livy! Livy!! Livy!!! It is widely known, for that pompous prig never misses the chance to tell anyone, that *he*, the great Livy, is working on the "definitive" history of Rome. Definitive my ass!

As if that fraud actually *knew* anything about the history of Rome! Oh, he talks a good game, I'll give him that. That insolent pup has become the darling of the so-called elite, who fawn over his every word as they sit around on their fat asses gorging themselves on fancy wine and cheese. How they go on and on about this so-called "history" of his, even though no one's actually *seen* a word. But I have something that young, bloodless simp could never have. You see dear reader—I was there!

Yes, I was there at the beginning. Well not actually at the *very* beginning, for it was my father who was with Aeneas and his original band of Trojans. But I was young man, no more than a stripling, a mere lad, when called upon to answer the call to duty by Rome—by joining in the rape of the Sabine women.

Part 2

LET THE GAMES BEGIN

As you know, after his brother's death, Romulus took steps to fortify the Palantine, and in no time the fortress had grown into his new city on the hill—Rome. It was Romulus who divided the army into cohorts of one hundred men, and assigned a captain to each—the first Centurions. He also created the senators, thus bestowing upon us our first politicians—a dubious achievement. Still, Romulus knew that it took more than strong walls, a disciplined army, and a ruling class to build a flourishing state. Since Rome was founded by the remnants of the Trojan army, it remained a masculine state with manly virtues. But the shortage of women was so serious that it was obvious: Rome's new-found strength would last no more than a single generation unless something drastic was done to replenish the population.

At first, King Romulus tried diplomacy. He sent envoys to all the peoples of Latinus to forge marriage alliances, but the petty chieftains who ruled the neighboring states were suspicious. Fearful of Rome and its growing might; they spurned our offers, and rudely sent our envoys packing. Particularly insulting was the message that came back from the officious Sabines: "If the sons of the Trojans were to spend more time at the altar of Venus and less time at the altar of Mars, heaven might send them more women."

On hearing this news, certain senators immediately urged that raids be mounted. We would abduct their women, and forcibly carry the captives off to Rome. But Romulus kept his own counsel. He was thinking on a grander scale than gaining a handful of women by a few scattered raids on local villages. Although we didn't know it, even then he had his eye on the Sabines, who were widely regarded as having the world's most beautiful women.

The Sabine women were striking: tall and well-built, with pleasing features, luxurious dark hair, and flashing eyes. These were alluring women whose passions were easily aroused, and whose lusty appetites were legendary among the peoples of Latinus. Sabine men, on the other had, tended to be meek and mild, scrawny in build, and easily dominated by their untamed women. They were duplicitous, indecisive, and prone to endless debate. They loved gossip as much as the Greeks, but talk alone seemed to satisfy them; they seldom rose to resolute action. Such pathetic males made poor warriors, and even more dubious allies. It was said that in the Sabine home, the woman ruled and the man dutifully obeyed—a situation any son of the Trojans would have found intolerable! Sabine men were weak as water, even as their women were strong and fiercely independent. It was widely rumored that the men were hardly up to the task of satisfying the voracious appetites of their highly-sensual mates.

There was another quality of the Sabines that would prove useful to the scheming Romulus. Like all Latin peoples, they were superstitious and deeply religious; far more afraid of offending any one of a hundred gods than they were of insulting the upstart King of Rome. Romulus devised a brilliant strategy that played upon this religious fervor. The King decided to use the feast of Consualia, held in honor of Neptune each year, to bring all the Sabine women we would need to Rome.

A large field had been cleared among the olive groves that spread out just below the city. It was on this grassy plain that the army exercised, honing their skills in endless war games. This same "Field of Mars" was used each spring for the festival of Consualia. Tents were set up; a miniature city grew up overnight.

Invitations were sent to all the Latin peoples, and they came in droves. In this festive atmosphere, men brought their families: women and children. And of course, we scanned the hordes of visitors, always on the alert for the most desirable womenfolk. It mattered not if she were a sturdy peasant girl who would make an agreeable wife for one of our soldier-farmers, or a high born lady, the sleek, attractive female from some minor aristocracy, destined to become the prized possession of one of our nobles. Young and old, wives and daughters, mistresses and concubines, even nubile slave girls, well-trained to please their wealthy masters, were all carefully studied with avid interest by the female-starved race of warriors that looked down upon the parade of visitors from their vantage point high atop the walls of Rome.

It was a brilliant day. A smiling sun shone down on the waiting throng, as Cletus, our chief priest, mounted a high wooden altar to stand flanked between two torches. In his dark fringe-lined toga, he appeared solemn and full of self-importance as he announced that, just as the Greeks were able to put aside their petty quarrels to come together in the spirit of the games, all able-bodied men would this year be asked to surrender their arms. They would be held in safe-keeping in one of the tents for the duration of the games.

Now, it was well known that at these annual festivals, the wine flowed freely, and petty quarrels inevitably broke out between our hot-blooded neighbors, usually with bloody consequences. Fights over women were common. And the mutual suspicion in which the states held each other, was not helped by the spirited games where rival champions were cheered on by excited and well-lubricated fans who had wagered heavily on their favorites. Cletus, Romulus' favorite priest, now informed the masses that such drunken brawls in which bones were broken and blood spilt, were profane to the honored god in whom name the festival was held. (A novel idea, I thought.) And to my astonishment, although not without a great deal of grumbling—the men grudgingly complied! Cletus waited until all the arms had been collected, and then with a sly smile, pronounced the official opening words: "Let the Games Begin!"

First up were the games—athletic contests that had become quite popular among our peoples wherein young men from the various tribes competed in trails of strength, speed, and agility. In keeping with the Greek tradition, the youthful athletes appeared for the contests totally nude, their hard sinewy bodies oiled, so that they gleamed in the afternoon sun as they paraded around before us.

They slowly marched in a single line to circle a dusty square, roped off as the arena for combat, and crowded with spectators on all four sides. The contestants were smiling and waving to the cheering crowd. There was a definite ripple of excitement that passed through the women in audience when the darkly handsome men of the Roman contingent strode by with their usual swagger, grinning and blowing kisses to their female admirers.

Part 3

SPECTATOR SPORTS

Still, I was paying little attention to those strutting exhibitionists, as my interest was inevitably drawn to the reactions of the women in the audience. My eye was caught by a bevy of delightful Sabine girls near the front row. They were crowded around two nobles seated on a low cushioned bench. I recognized the Sabine chieftain, an officious fussbudget named Tatius. To his left, sat an elegant lady of breathtaking beauty. In the midst of excitement, she maintained her poise, erect and serene, as if a little remote from the press of the rabble all around her. She might be nothing more than the consort of a petty chieftain, yet she held herself with the regal bearing of a queen. This could only be Cataluna—the Queen of the Sabines. A woman whose beauty was legendary. I studied her aristocratic features: those lovely eyes, the precisely etched lips, high cheekbones that gave that proud face a sculpted look.

Her long and slender body was draped in a loose shift of fine-spun linen that fell to her ankles. The narrow gown was slit up the sides to allow freedom of movement, and not incidentally an enticing glimpse of those exquisite legs of hers. I noticed that Tatius had laid his bony ringed figures on the lady's right thigh with a proprietary air, but she ignored his crude impertinence, reserving all her attention for the parade of naked men who now stood in a loose circle saluting the crowd.

For the next hour or so we were treated to various games—races, jumping contests, gymnastics, and the like. We watched the men straining and struggling in the hot sun, their well-oiled bodies glistening and sheened with sweat, locked in contests at which we Romans excelled. All of our able bodied men followed a regimen of physical fitness that began upon entering the army at age sixteen, and lasted throughout life, so many blue ribbons were to adorn Rome's banner that day.

It was when the wrestlers took the field that a trill of girlish laugher turned my attention to a flock of eager and excited young women nudging each other, snickering, and pointing in the most ribald manner. The object of their interest was one of our champions, Maximus, whose nickname in the army was "Penis Longa." The masculine equipment this stalwart displayed was oversized by any measure, one might even say, grotesque. And he made the most of his attributes by the way he strode wide-legged, letting it all sway before him. I glanced at Cataluna and saw a wicked gleam in her eyes and a thin smile on her lips. Tatius looked sour; his pinched face scowling.

A shrieking whoop came from the bevy of lightly-dressed girls, and I noticed one who was bouncing lightly on her tiptoes, flushed, and clapping her hands in girlish glee as Maximus acknowledged the accolades with a friendly wave. She and her sisters were clumped in the outer circle, a few rows back from where the high born nobles had ensconced themselves. Lithe and small breasted, she wore a thin Greek-style tunic that left her youthful arms and legs quite bare, and she had her shiny chestnut hair drawn back in a perky ponytail. As I stared at her, she happened to turn and our eyes met. She smiled.

I felt drawn to the pretty girl with the come-hither smile, which I took as an invitation. I moved over to be closer to this pert Sabine maiden. Edging up, I placed myself no more than a few inches behind her slight body and from there I could gaze down at her narrow shoulders, bare fragile shoulders looped with the thin straps of the tunic, and that neat ponytail which hung down only inches from my admiring eyes. I felt my penis stirring under my thin kilt. Scarcely daring to breathe, I widened my stance and waited for a surge in the crowd that would squeeze our congested bodies together. Then, at the moment when her soft bottom was inevitably pressed back into my loins, she turned to glance up over her shoulder. Her big brown eyes seemed to flicker with recognition, and she gave me a decidedly pleased smile.

There was a roar from the crowd as two wrestlers, one a muscular, long-armed guy from Arcia fell into the crouch of a big cat as he looked for an opening to close with a barrel-chested Remurian with a powerful build and a remarkably small penis, who scuttled around cautiously just outside his reach.

When my girl turned back to watch in rapt fascination as the two naked men grappled on the dusty field, I screwed up my courage and pressed my hips boldly forward bringing my thinly-clad erection into solid contact with her girlish bottom. And to my great delight the little minx, while never taking her wide eyes off the sweating men, wiggled her impertinent little ass back against me!

Thus began our own secret game, played within the game that was unfolding before us as the two wrestlers were now down on all fours. The Arcian was bent over under the weight of the heavier Remurian who arched over his back his thick arms locked around his opponent's heaving chest. The girl gasped and a hand flew to her gaping mouth as the nude wrestlers became a grunting beast with two backs.

I rubbed up against her, wiggled my hips letting my little Sabine get the full measure of my expanded cock against her thinly-clad bottom. She arched back against me, and a hand came back to clasp my thigh, as if to brace herself.

Then, wonder of wonders, that stealthy hand snaked between our tightly pressed bodies, the fingers groping blindly for my tented manhood. And when my Sabine vixen found my rock-hard penis, she closed on me and abruptly squeezed.

The brazen move tore a groan from my lips, causing our closely packed neighbors to give me a curious look. I managed a weak smile for the closest girlfriends, as the pressure of those gripping fingers eased —although they never totally gave up the prize she so obviously coveted.

My new playmate took a moment to fondle me through kilt and loincloth, then withdrew her wicked hand. By now I was hot, and eager to return the favor. I slipped a hand down to cup the girl's pert rearend, moving my hand over her thinly clad ass, giving her a squeeze through her skirt, then sliding the sheer fabric over that tight-cheeked young bottom.

She squirmed in the rising heat, ground her bottom into my hand, and gave such an excited wiggle that my already hard prick surged with intolerable readiness.

My hand moved in a heated rush, sliding down to fumble for the hem of the short tunic were it rested half way down her thigh, to touch her on the bare leg and then to slip up under the little skirt for a journey of discovery. As I suspected, the saucy girl wore no loincloth and I was now treated to the smooth feel of her bare bottom. I let her little rump fill my palm and closed my fingers to grab a handful of those hard young cheeks.

The girl's buttocks clenched, tightened down. She gasped and jerked upright. Suddenly, her hand flew back, clamped my wrist and drew my hand from under her skirt. Still held by the hand, I was dragged after the excited girl as she pushed her way through the crowd intent on finding some privacy within the olive groves far from the roaring crowd.

And it was there that the girl flung herself at me with opened legs that clamped my hips, and greedy thighs that drew me to her in repeated lusty spasms. History may credit Romulus, but I can assure you that Plunar and Lolatina (for such was my Sabine playmate's name) were the first to unite Romans and the Sabines.

Part 4
OUR CHAMPION RAISES HIS MIGHTY SWORD

The sun was low in the west by the time Lolatina and I were able to rejoin the crowd, earning some knowing glances from her girlfriends who now huddled around her, eager for the whispered news. Unlike some of the other women of the Latin tribes, these Sabines showed not the slightest reluctance in openly discussing their sexual activities and the performance of their mates, and while not privy to the enthusiastic feminine discussion that now bubbled up all around me, I did find myself favored with frequent smiles of approval as pretty heads turned my way. For my part, I tried to ignore the flurry of hushed conversations and girlish giggles, although I was well aware of the lewd glances, even though I kept my gaze to the front, determined to concentrate on the arena.

We had arrived back just in time for the war games, mock battles in which champions were chosen from each of the neighboring states to compete with wooden weapons upon the field of battle.

I noticed the regal Cataluna now sat under a shade of awning that had been erected for the nobles, while at her side her bumbling, complaining husband fussed over the accommodations. The Lady paid not the slightest attention to him, but sat upright and erect, her keenly interested gaze locked on the two combatants who now took the field: Tacitus, our mighty Roman hero, and Nereus, the formidable giant who was the champion of the Gabii. The crowd greeted the popular heroes with a lusty roar. I stole a glance at Lola whose eyes were shining with excitement, and then at the Lady, whose gaze seemed cooler, but no less interested.

Now she straightened in her seat and leaned slightly forward, her eyes eager and alert, as our champion, Tacitus strode onto the hard dusty field. His tight muscular body was lightly clad in a sleeveless leather jerkin; a short warrior's kilt that left exposed the hard sinewy legs and powerful hairy thighs of our stalwart hero; his only armor was the bronze helmet of the Trojans, and the gleaming metal breastplate. As we watched, the two combatants drew the wooden swords slung into their belts, and brought them up in salute to the crowd. The crowd went wild.

Once again the deadly dance ensued, although this time the man-to-man ballet included weapons, the wily opponents circled, each looking for his advantage. And when the fight was joined there was a mad scramble of limbs and swinging swords. It happened so fast that it was hard to follow the action. Nereus gained the initial advantage, pressed his attack, drove Tacitius backward, and the Roman stumbled.

The Romans in the crowd let out a fearful groan. Cataluna jerked upright in her chair, a hand came up in shocked surprise to flutter in the air.

Nereus was relentless, seizing the opportunity to lung forward, but in the nick of time the crafty Roman had regained his stance just enough to evade the thrusting sword and to deliver instead his own blow that caught Nereus on the side of the helmet. We heard the crack through the crowd, and that solid smack caused the charging Nereus to falter. He shook his head like a mad bull and charged forward, constantly attacking. But if Nereus relied on his brute strength, Tacitus had the advantage of the more skillful adept moves of an expert swordsman. He danced out of the way of a sweeping scythe, ducked over the wavering sword, and in one smooth movement, thrust forward to punch his wooden weapon right into the underbelly of his opponent, sinking in the blunted point just below the protective breastplate. The brute's eyes bulged out and his mouth gaped open as his sword fell and he clutched his stomach with both hands. Winded, he fell to his knees, gaping like a newly-caught fish.

The crowd cheered, and the usually cool Queen of the Sabines joined right in, bouncing up in her cheering and waving her fists in the air, while her disapproving husband leaned back to regard this display of girlish enthusiasm with grim censure.

Meanwhile, Tacitus had deftly stepped behind his winded opponent and while Nereus was still on his knees, powerful chest heaving as he struggled for breath, Tacitus whacked him on the back his helmeted head with a blow that rang out over the crowd. Nereus fell forward, crashing down like a mighty oak; Tacitus raised a sandaled foot and placed it lightly on the neck of his fallen foe.

The crowd roared its approval, cheering wildly, and I saw the flushed and excited Lady Cataluna jump to her feet clapping with wild abandon at the mighty warrior who now looked her way and gave, just to her—or so it seemed to me, a nod and a huge grin of triumph.

⎯⎯⎯⎯⎯∞⎯⎯⎯⎯⎯

These heated contests were a great success with the crowd, and they were followed by a night of feasting and drinking and merrymaking. The women of each tribe took turns presenting their traditional dances, but it was the lithe Sabine girls who performed bare breasted, their supple bodies clad in nothing but skimpy loincloths, who were the most admired for their lively performance. They bounded with surprising agility and natural grace, twisting and turning their nubile young bodies, tumbling like acrobats, whirling and leaping with athletic ease in an energetic display that had the crowd breathless.

It was hardly surprising that the acrobatic dances of such scantily clad girls would instantly stir the passions of every red-blooded Roman. Their show was greeted by thunderous applause, and Romans rushed forward bringing offerings of wine to the sweating, panting dancers. After that spirited dance it was inevitable that Roman men and Sabine women should become much better acquainted. We soon found that these Sabines lived up to their reputations as highly-sexed women. They were outrageous flirts who thoroughly relished a good roll in the hay; fidelity to husbands, and even fathers, were not among their strongly held virtues.

Romulus was a generous host; our wine is the finest, and it flowed freely that night. Under the glow of torches one could see the revelers growing more brazenly amorous. The firelight showed warm faces with flushed cheeks and eyes that shone with excitement. Clothes were being shed with careless disregard, while eager hands explored freely. Half-naked women were locked in torrid embraces with fully clothed soldiers; nude girls climbed all over supine partners who still might retain a kilt or loincloth, if that. Naked men danced around the campfires, or strode about looking for conquests with erected penises at the ready. Women sported excited nipples that blossomed forth in the first flush of excitement. Sensitive to warm summer's night that seemed redolent of sex, such thickened nipples stuck out in brazen display, their tips stiff with arousal.

I managed to find my Lola, and in a heated rush we raced back to the woods, only to find them populated with new-found lovers who had paired off and were now eagerly exploring the magic of warm summer nights in the moonlit olive groves. Coupling couples were strewn about every-where. Grunts and moans, the sounds of love came from all directions, as eager lovers gave and took the pleasures of lips and mouths and tongues. Even as some amorous couples made their way to more secluded places, those who were bolder, burning with impatience, or simply more inebriated, were having sex openly in the most public of places.

A well-known senator sat ensconced on a small camp chair. At his feet, a naked women sat back on her folded legs. She had his loincloth shoved back, his penis exposed. She held his manhood at the base with a clenched fist, and she was slowly, languidly licking up and down its quivering length with the soft lapping strokes of a big cat. The man groaned, leaned back, and shuddered with pleasure. A com-panion of his sat in an identical chair beside him. In his lap a sensual raven haired beauty sat facing him, her dangling legs straddling his thighs. His hands came around to cup her bounding ass, as this magnificent animal bobbed up and down on his upright penis, flinging her long heavy mane in wild abandon, while he arched back straining up to meet her as she fucked the seated man with lusty enthusiasm.

As we made our way through clusters of revelers, Lola moved closer to me, took my arm, linked it through hers. The nearness of this naked girl at my side had me tingling with excitement. Under my loincloth, my erection had become impossibly stiff.

A tall rangy man was taking a woman from behind, having placed her on hands and knees. She was a big, fleshy girl with velvety golden skin, a wide, generous bottom, and rich succulent tits that hung down heavily below her bent torso. He held her by her sturdy hips as he pumped into her with slow deep, measured strokes. As we watched, the couple fell into a jogging rhythm that sent her dangling breasts swinging, while she shook her head and clenched her teeth at each savage thrust of his relentless cock.

With a cup of wine in one hand, I ran the other down the smooth back of slender Lola who pressed her nude body up against me and snuggled up with her head on my shoulders. As we watched the two lovers, Lola brought a thin arm around to run a hand down between our tightly-pressed bodies, impishly seeking my manhood, and she fondled me while we watched.

For my part, I couldn't keep my hands off the girl. I let my hand slide down to cup her sweet little bottom, and she strained up on tip toes to reach my lips. We kissed—a passionate, open-mouthed kiss of burgeoning power. Her soft nude body melted into mine, and I held her tight. When we broke apart, we continued our stroll, with arms loosely slung around each other—a couple of lovers, threading their way through an orgy of lust.

We heard a keening screech of passion, like a banshee in heat, and turned to see, from behind a bush, a pair of long, white, decidedly feminine legs sticking up in the air and fluttering madly in the moonlight, before they clamped down around the pumping waist of a stalwart warrior who had plunged in to bury himself between the lady's hungry thighs. As we drew closer, the shock of recognition came over me. We were watching none other than the Lady Cataluna being lustily fucked by our champion, the indomitable Tacitus.

For a while we stood entranced, watching the couple furiously fuck, then Lola laughed her low earthy laugh and made a grab for my crotch. Clasping me by the prick, she dragged me along to a grassy knoll.

I had my playmate sprawled out on her back, her legs widespread, and I was kneeling between her splayed thighs, weapon in hand and a single purpose in mind, when we heard a terrible commotion. Men were shouting, women shrieking in fear and outrage. Then a gang of men were running past us. Lightly-clad but undoubtedly Roman soldiers, they carried with them into the woods a clump of protesting Sabine women.

We later learned that, after some slight, real or imagined, there had been a raid on the Sabine camp. It seems a few of our lads who were well in their cups and lacking female companionship, decided to hunt for Sabine women who had held back from the merry-making, spurning the advances of Roman men by retreating to their tents. When the amorous Romans pursued these reluctant virgins, they were turned away by the sober Sabine elders. This, they decided, was an insult to Roman hospitality, and they decided it was their duty to help the pretty ladies overcome their shyness. The drunken louts found the first tent they came to, one that, unbeknownst to them housed his lordship Tatius, his family, and certain of his nobles. And it was upon these worthies that the drunken Romans crashed in. The marauders attacked the men in a general brawl (weapons you may remember had been banned, but our boys made a good account of themselves using their fists and whatever came to hand). With the men temporarily laid out, the raiders set upon the women, who they dragged kicking and screaming into the woods.

This was the gang that thundered past us as we lay on the grass. I managed to get up on one elbow enough to see the retreating figure of a nearly-naked man, humping along with a large woman thrown over his shoulder like sack of grain. She was hollering, cursing him, and kicking wildly as he carried her off. The shrieks of outrage merged into the general cacophony, mingling with the screams of ecstatic delight that resounded in that holy grove.

———✆———

Throughout the night, virile Romans and healthy Sabines coupled with reckless abandon, often under the very noses of spineless husbands and ineffectual fathers who had no hope of controlling such red-blooded and impetuous females. And thus the festive evening degenerated into a full-blown midnight orgy.

Part 5
THE RAPE (OR SOMETHING VERY MUCH LIKE IT)

Dawn marked the official end of the festival; the dew was burning off the campgrounds, and tents were being struck with the rising sun. The hung-over crowds began to slowly disperse, the clans packing up and making their way back to their ancestral homes—all, that is, but the Sabines. They stayed behind, huddled in council. After several hours, a delegation was sent to seek an immediate audience with Romulus. These worthies pronounced themselves shocked and outraged at the flagrant sexual behavior of their hosts, and they demanded an apology. The Romans had been insensitive—even carrying off their women into the woods! Others also complained of what they called sexual harassment; the women being subject to lewd remarks and rough treatment at the hands of the Romans. The haughty Tatius, quivering in righteous indignation, couldn't help hinting that, along with the apology, perhaps some Roman gold might help to erase the insult to Sabine honor.

Romulus listened patiently. He said that he was shocked

to hear that his men had behaved so badly. Moreover he wished to punish any wrongdoers. But first the women who had been wronged must be brought forth as witnesses. He must hear their tales of being used so shamelessly from their very own lips before making his judgment. He suggested that the entire clan be assembled in the Forum so he might hear their grievances. Apologies, and even the matter of restitution, he hinted with a sly smile, might then be discussed.

Accordingly, that very afternoon, the horde of Sabines made their trek up the hill and passed under the walls and through the city gates to meet with our king. Once the last of our guests had assembled under the vaulted ceilings of the great hall, a group of the palace guards in full battle array slipped into the room by a hidden entrance, and quickly and quietly barred each of the doors.

The Sabines looked about uneasily, mumbling to themselves in growing consternation, till they were silenced by the sudden appearance of Romulus, flanked by his centurions and looking quite splendid in full armor with the wreath of golden laurel leaves he always wore when he sat in judgment. The room fell silent as he ascended to the rostra, and then paused to address the assembled throng. The speech our monarch now delivered was clear and direct, and not at all what our guests expected to hear.

He had heard wild stories of the happenings in the olive groves last night, drunken revelries carried on right under the very nose of the god on this most holiest of feast days. He paused; the Sabines looked up at him, nodding and expectant.

He now continued. But because the sinners had not been struck down in rightful wrath, his priest assured him, the benevolence showed that this was clearly a sign from heaven. He looked at his high priest, Cletus, who dutifully nodded his long bald head in agreement. Indeed, the gods must have been pleased. In this puzzling situation, he had made offerings and consulted the oracle. The answer was plain: It could only be the will of the god Neptune— Roman men and Sabine women should be as one! The god therefore would guide their deliberations as they now selected one third of the Sabine women to stay behind to join in creating a great race of warriors.

At these words, the singing of a hundred swords being drawn from metal lined scabbards hissed through the quiet room, and the Sabines quickly looked around them to see the fully-armed soldiers holding their weapons at the ready. Now, for the first time, the Sabine men fully realized their predicament. They had foolishly allowed themselves to fall, unarmed, into the hands of their bitter rivals, and could only escape with their lives if they acquiesced to the outrageous demand now put to them so calmly by the smiling King of the Romans.

When they got over their shocked surprise, the leaders of the Sabines began to clamor all at once. Romulus let the cacophony of outraged voices grow to hysterical proportions, he then held up a single hand to silence them. Then he turned his back on his audience, climbed the few steps to his throne, and sat down to face them once again. The King always took the throne when he was to make judicial judgments. I still remember his speech to the Sabines: "This is a sign from heaven, and so it cannot be ignored. As all pious people know, those who would spurn the will of the gods do so at their own peril. The King and Senate of Rome has no choice therefore, but to follow the will of the gods." And then he paused, and smiled straight at the seething Tatius. "Perhaps if the Sabines had spent more time standing before the altar of Mars and less time prostrating themselves before their women, they might still have their women."

∞∞∞

Those of us who were there that day well remember the sight of that the sorry procession of defeated men with the few remaining women allowed to them, clinging to each other as they made their way down the hill from the city to the jeers of the armed solders who stood looking down on them from the ramparts. Few of us who watched from the walls believed the Sabines would suffer this defeat without an attempt to win back their women, once they had rearmed and regrouped.

But for now Romulus turned to the task at hand. Well aware that this sudden windfall of desirable women would spark jealousy, and possibly even bloodletting among the Romans, he had devised a system for dividing up the spoils of our (so far) bloodless conquest. Once the sorry troop had been disposed of, the remaining women were herded into the center of the great hall, and there they were ordered to undress.

Each rank of citizens would be allowed to select in turn: after the king, would come the senators, followed by centurions, soldiers, craftsmen, and farmers. Within each rank, the women were to be chosen by lot. It was later rumored that some of our wealthier senators had manipulated the drawings, assuring they would get the handful of women they lusted after, and enforcing their choices by entering the hall accompanied by their own gangs of hired thugs.

We watched with interest as the abducted women began slowly to undress. Most were frightened; many were resigned, almost morose—but the full range of human emotions could be seen in their faces. Some were crying and seeking comfort in each other's arms. Mothers held their daughters; sisters wiped the tears of younger sisters. Other girls, made of sterner stuff, prepared themselves to meet their fate with stoic resolve. They would make the best Roman mothers, or so it seemed to me. And here and there one could discern, from a sly glance or a twinkle in the eye, that the prospect of being taken by the Romans was not all together displeasing . . . not at all.

With their clothes disposed of, the nude captives were made to line up in cohorts of one hundred, to present themselves while the king and nobility of Rome slowly trooped the rows of Sabine beauties, selecting those from among them who would serve as wives, concubines, or even slaves. Motionless the women waited, standing at attention with chins held high, shoulders back, and breasts proudly displayed as they awaited male inspection.

While the very old and the very young had been allowed to leave, the remainder represented a wide variety of females in all shapes and sizes. There were girls and maidens, and young women, as well as those more mature females who were well into their child-bearing years.

There were tall girls and short girls; thin slightly-built girls with long straight limbs, and pleasingly curved girls, curvaceous and sassy. There were sturdy women, and big women, voluptuous, with impressive statuesque bodies. Some had long hair; some short hair. There were those who wore their hair cropped neatly short, or in soft waves, or in masses of curls, or in straight, smooth sheets of fine-spun silk; all colors and tints and hues of hair were represented.

Each man who passed by had the opportunity to leisurely admire each and every woman, and of course the nearness of such feminine beauty invited the masculine hand to partake of a sample.

A man might cup a jutting breast, lifting up some rich, full bosom to finger the soft silky flesh before allowing it to settle into place with a shimmy evocative of richly laden promise. Or a pair of girlish tits might draw one's attention, young hard breasts that stick right out at you with saucy impudence. There were wobbly, flattened-mounds to be admired; and floppy little titties that jiggled with delight. There were perky tits; firm, jellied mounds which make tidy handfuls; or flat-chested girls—with hopeful nascent titties emergent on their slim, maidenly chests. Nipples came in for a lot of attention. Some were highly responsive; awakening and blossoming with just the slightest bit of fingering. There were nipples that lie crinkled in quiet repose, or jutted out—stiffly protruding after having been coaxed into arousal. Ones that are big and fat with wide disks of aureolae smiling at you; or small and precise nipples, buttons of fleshy pink, dusky, or rich chocolatety brown.

Hands caressed sensuous contours of the long lovely legs, slender legs; shapely legs that parted instinctively so that those loving hands could savor the silken skin of smooth tapering thighs. Fondling hands fully and deeply explored naked feminine bottoms, appraising high-set cheeks, and shapely behinds, finding delight in pleasantly plump bottoms, tight-cheeked young bottoms. Who could help but to want to test the bouncy pliancy of a set of impertinent buttocks that wobbled tautly after each playful smack?

Insatiable male hands were thoroughly enjoying the delights to be found in fondling naked female flesh. The seductive curves of attractive legs, long tapering limbs, were thoroughly explored by slow hands making their leisurely journey of sensual delight. Bouncy, elegant rearcheeks were touched and held, lavishly felt up, their firm resiliency tested by masculine hands that cupped and squeezed. Naked haunches were adored by appreciative hands that took their pleasure in the sleek, smooth feel of those delicious contours.

Here and there some horny connoisseur might pause to test his partner's sexual responsiveness. A tall lanky girl with a mane of thick dark hair, and delicate, teardrop shaped breasts, struggled to maintain her composure while an affectionate admirer subjected every inch of her healthy young body to most exquisite, tantalizing caresses.

Another man might trace the slope of a fully curved breast belonging to a big curvaceous woman, fingering the firmly rounded, outthrust mound before testing its taut elasticity by gently tugging on a nipple. He would enjoy playing her body like a fine instrument, plucking that prominent nipple that expanded under his touch, toying with it, while the big woman, wiggled her shoulders and writhed under all this attention. Still another man might slip a hand around to explore the behind of a young woman whose tight-cheeked ass he fully expected to enjoy. She would try to hold the mandated pose with hands at her side, while he insinuated a single finger between her clamping cheeks and probed wickedly in that most intimate of places.

While most of the captives were cooperative to some degree during, what might be for them a trying ordeal, some of the more prideful women made their resentment known. The ones that remained stubborn and all together too arrogant were made to assume more blatantly suggestive poses to the amusement of the leering men. They had to raise their hands, link their fingers behind the nape of the neck, and thrust their chests forward for detailed examination. They had to bend over and reach behind to open their cheeks for further inspection. Those who refused, were reminded of the price of disobedience by guards who ominously carried short, light-weight whips. A whipping bite across the buttocks could bring instant compliance from all but the most recalcitrant females.

Special treatment was reserved for the aristocrats who proved particularly haughty, their manner showing that they clearly saw the Romans as crude upstarts. Such a lady might be forced to her knees and ordered to masturbate for the amusement of the ribald crowd. She might equally be forced to pay tribute to a dangling Roman rod, while she was cheered on in her efforts.

The slow parade of men made their way into the Forum to troop the rows of increasingly excited women selecting one or two who caught their fancy, and then hurrying home with women in tow to try out their latest acquisitions.

Part 6

THE WOMEN'S REVOLT

Several weeks went by as we waited for an attack of the Sabine army, who everyone knew would try to take back their women. But there was no sign of them, and with each passing day things became a little less tense. The abducted women were settling in to their new roles; many seemed to have accepted their fate, and at least a handful seemed quite content with these new arrangements. They were discovering that Roman men were, after all, not without their charms.

Romulus did his part in helping them to accept the inevitable, visiting with each of them in turn, promising they would enjoy all the privileges of married Romans, and that, in time, they would come to care for husbands, hearth, and children. The lands of Rome were rich and fertile, virgin fields that and could yield abundant crops. The mighty Roman Legions would protect the city and its homes, and bring back booty and riches from foreign conquests far and wide. In time, Rome would grow rich and prospectus, and this was the future he now offered to them. Romulus was a very persuasive speaker.

And as the months went on, the women lost much of their resentment and began to build new lives with their Roman mates. But our spies told us the Sabine men were far from resigned. Rumors persisted that an army under their commander, Mettus Curtius, had been assembled and would soon be ready to march on Rome.

But while some degree of domestic peace seemed to have taken root in our city, not all the women accepted their new status. Not all, by any means. Some remained furious and obstinate, seething with deep resentment of their Roman overlords. And first among those who agitated for return to their ancestral lands was a certain Lavinia, a magnificent woman of hot temper and overweening pride, who often boasted that no Roman could ever tame her. She had been claimed by Turnus, a competent enough com- mander in the field, but one who remained at a loss as to how to deal with the firecat he had on his hands.

Romulus kept a wary eye on her. That woman had a commanding presence, he was heard to say, and must be tamed, or else she would surely stir up trouble.

But if the Sabines were making preparations for war, we ourselves were far from idle. Romulus had ordered a citadel to be built guarding the approach to the city. The citadel would be a key outpost, his best men placed there under the able command of Surius Tarpeius. This new brick fortress was completed just in time for our spies reported that the Sabine army had began to march.

Mettus came upon the citadel and immediately realized the road to Rome would be blocked unless he could first overcome this stronghold. During several days of bloody fighting, determined Sabine attacks were repeatedly beaten back, but then the Sabines resorted to a ruse.

It so happened that a handful of Roman girls had fallen under the evil influence of Lavinia. These young maidens were chronically discontent, seething under real and imagined slights by what they saw as the overbearing males in their lives. Lavinia played upon this smoldering adolescent discontent and fanned the flames of rebellion. It was no surprise that these girls were also deeply jealous of the lovely Sabines, resenting the men for bringing the newcomers into their midst.

Here too, Lavinia suggested they could make common cause—by helping the Sabine army to retrieve their women. Now among those who were in league with Lavinia, was a certain Tarepeia, who happened to be the daughter of Trapieus, commander of the citadel.

A plot was laid, whereby one night, at a pre-arranged signal, Tarepeia would open a small gate in the rear wall to let the invaders into the fortress. The ploy was wholly successful, and what Mettus could not take gain by storm he was able to take by guile.

When Romulus found out his men had been betrayed, he was furious. The plot was quickly uncovered and the traitors rounded up. Four women were implicated: Lavinia, Tarepeia, Rhea, and Caecilia, the latter two were daughters of wealthy families. Rhea's father was a patrician; Caecilia was the silly, idle daughter of a senator.

Romulus decreed that the plotters be publicly punished for their treachery, and that all citizens should gather in the Forum to witness their punishment.

The three girls were stripped of their garments and led naked to the dusty square at the center of the Forum. There they were forced to lay face down, and stretch out their limbs so that they could be tied down naked to the stakes that had been driven into the ground. Now their fathers were handed switches and they proceed to administer the public punishment, whapping their daughters' aristocratic behinds with thin whippy rods while the hills rang to the echoing wails of the sobbing miscreants. Such punishment was deemed proper, for these foolish girls had betrayed Rome, and brought dishonor upon the family name.

For Lavinia, Romulus had reserved a special punishment. One he would personally administer. The Sabine woman was led naked onto a raised platform and there bent over a sturdy crossbar, her hands down in front of her and fastened to the floor, while she was drawn up onto her toes, with her rich full bottom properly exposed and positioned for chastisement. Romulus took a position behind the naked woman, and with a well chosen scourge began to lash that worthy's upraised rump to the wild applause of the rabble.

***

Now Romulus took steps to meet the Sabine challenge. He would personally lead the rest of our army into battle. After occupying the citadel, the Sabines moved down to meet the advancing Romans. In the ensuing melee, Mettus narrowly saved himself from sinking into a swamp, and the battle was continuing on the low ground when the Sabine women intervened. They charged onto the field and imposed their bodies between the combatants, appealing for them to stop fighting. The effect of this appeal was miraculous and a moment later Romulus and Mettus stepped forward to make peace. And from that day on the two peoples were combined as one, under the eagle of Rome.

———⸺———

These are the fact, even if they are obscured by Livy's turgid prose. Yes, Livy has completed his account of our history and has taken to reading from it each day at the Forum. The man is self-serving and insufferable. Still his work is widely heralded and the Roman mobs are thrilled to hear about the glorious deeds of their ancestors. Livy is an outrageous flatterer, and I caution you dear reader, not one to be believed.